The Moon Goddess

A Teen Wolf FanFiction

Michael E. Sweeny

Table Of Contents

CHAPTER 1

It was calm at Beacon Hills. But Beacon Hills wouldn't be Beacon Hills if something horrible wasn't already waiting again for the pack. Maybe Stiles should have urged his parents to relocate to another state or maybe to another country. He should have done it the second he found out that his closest buddy was a raging werewolf. But then, it would not have been Stiles' life and Stiles wouldn't be Stiles.

"Do you think I should call her or something? I don't know what we are, I mean, are we a thing now? Like a genuine thing?", Scott remarked uneasily and gazed out of the jeep's window into the dark. There were showers on the windows and it was impossible to see anything through all the rain.

"Maybe you should simply ask her what she wants?", Stiles said and moved his head away from the road for a brief second to gaze at his closest buddy. Scott tilted his head to meet

Stiles's gaze and stared at him with his are-you-serious face.

"Don't look at me like that, guy. You're the one asking me for relationship advice. You know, particularly me. I went after one lady for four years and didn't even have a chance when her nasty boyfriend moved to the other side of the planet. You shouldn't expect any relationship advice from me.", Stiles murmured and focused back on the dark road in front of him. Scott shrugged his shoulders and let his head fall on the seat.

"Stiles, watch out!", he immediately cried as he noticed something lying on the road. Stiles instantly slammed the brakes of the jeep and the automobile unexpectedly halted. The two of them merely gazed at the girl lying on the road for a few seconds before Scott eventually came back to his senses and hopped out of the vehicle. Even Stiles found himself thinking straight again and raced after Scott who was now kneeling close to the girl.

"Is she hurt?", Stiles inquired out of breath when he finally approached Scott and the girl. Scott kneeled on the damp road and peered at the girl with burning red eyes and furrowed eyebrows.

"I'm not sure. I don't see or smell any blood. We should take her to the hospital anyhow.", Scott said gently and lifted part of the golden hair off the girl's face.

"Hey, I know her. That's Selena Wilson. She was at the Eichen House.", Stiles observed and felt how his pulse instantly sped up. Stiles stepped closer to the girl and squatted next to her, so he could see her better through the rain. The girl was just wearing a white medical gown and her virtually white hair appeared black from the rain.

"They detained her.", Stiles stated softly and spotted the purple and black bruises on her wrists and ankles.

"Let's go.", Scott stated severely and scooped the child up to carry her in his arms. Scott brought the child to the vehicle and set her down in the backseat gently. They both hopped into their seats and headed to the Beacon Hills Memorial Hospital. Just as previously, Stiles applied the brakes and the vehicle halted unexpectedly. Scott pulled the child back in his arms and brought her inside of the hospital with a miraculous speed. Stiles only prayed that nobody would notice.

"Mum, she needs assistance!", Scott cried in the direction of his mother who was seated at the registration counter. Melissa rose and accompanied Scott into one of the rooms where he set her down on a hospital bed.

"What happened?", Melissa inquired and was already examining the girls' hearts and lungs after she notified a doctor.

"We don't know. She was resting on the road but I can't smell any damage. She's from the Eichen House.", Scott stated and Melissa nodded her head as she placed a touch on the girl's forehead to test her body temperature.

"She's hypothermic but appears to be stable. Scott, go to the reception and ask for blankets and when a doctor will be here." Scott merely nodded and exited the room. Stiles was standing there, still perplexed and horrified when he observed the ladies' lips becoming blue.

"Oh, here you go. That could help a bit.", Stiles remarked and took off his jacket. Melissa grabbed the jacket from his hands and smiled at him pleasantly before she draped the jacket over the girl's body to keep her warm. Melissa grabbed a tiny flashlight and leaned over the girl to examine the function of her pupils. She opened the girls' eyelids with her fingers slowly but suddenly Stiles and Melissa both shied away with a startled look on their faces.

"What is happening?", Scott inquired who unexpectedly entered the room and found his closest buddy and mother with horrified looks.

"Her eyes were shining.", Melissa merely replied and glanced at the girl with large eyes.

"She's a werewolf? But I can't smell her.", Scott merely muttered and glanced at the girl with a bewildered face.

"No, buddy. Her eyes were flashing silver." The guys knew about the distinct tints of werewolf eyes. They have seen golden eyes, blue eyes, and crimson eyes. But silver eyes? Well, that was new.

"Stiles. Stiles, wake up." Stiles startled, lost his balance and slowly slipped off the little chair.

"You dad is come to take you up. You should go home and get some rest.", Melissa suggested and stared at him with a troubled face. It was the same attitude his mother often used to gaze at him when he was upset or unwell. Melissa undoubtedly was like a second mother to Stiles. Stiles rose and wiped his eyes with his hands.

"I believe someone should be present when she wakes up. She doesn't have any relatives. Did someone contact the Eichen House already? She shouldn't go back, they detained her.",

Stiles hurriedly babbled and gazed at the girl with sleepy eyes. Underneath the covers, Stiles could see the sleeve of this garment. He was becoming chilly by now but of course, he would not confess it and beg for his jacket. The girls' hair dried and appeared blonde again. Nearly white. Just how Stiles might remember it. Stiles was confident of the fact, that this was Selena Wilson sleeping in front of him.

"We did not call them yet. Your father knows everything and will try his utmost to keep them away from her. Scott requested Deaton to care after her but he's out of town till tomorrow morning. What do you know about her, Stiles? Why was she at the Eichen House?"

"I don't know anything about her. We had a couple of group sessions together. Her parents died a few years ago and she faced a lot of emotional breakdowns." Melissa nodded in agreement and gazed at Selena with sorrowful eyes. Her physical circumstances became better and her body temperature went back to normal but it still didn't look, like she was going to wake up any time soon. Stiles massaged his sleepy eyes when the door slowly opened and this dad entered the room.

"Hey, son. My shift is finished, let's go home.", his dad replied and proceeded farther into the room. Stiles gazed at Selena and didn't know what to do. She should not wake up and be alone, nobody should go through anything like that on their alone.

"I suppose I will remain here. She shouldn't be alone when she wakes up.", Stiles responded and stared at his dad. The sheriff pinched his lips together, not sure whether he should attempt to sway his son's opinion or not. He opted not to and merely nodded, knowing he didn't have a chance anyhow.

"I will bring you some food tomorrow morning before my shift begins.", were the last words the sheriff said before he bid goodbye and left the hospital.

"Where's Scott by the way?", Stiles suddenly realized and turned his focus back to Melissa who shrugged her shoulders.

"He wanted to visit Derek to question him about Selena and the silver eyes. He departed approximately two hours ago after you fell asleep.". Stiles grabbed his phone and noticed that there were no missed calls or messages. He narrowed his eyes and let himself fall back on the chair. After Melissa left the room, Stiles felt a horrible sensation in his stomach. Something didn't feel right here. Scott was gone for two hours and didn't contact Stiles yet. If Derek would have known anything, Scott would have at least contacted Stiles already and if Derek would not know anything, Scott would be back already. Stiles's tense fingers moved across the display of his phone as he dialed Scott. He didn't anticipate Scott to take his phone, but he left a message in his mailbox regardless.

"You better have a solid reason for all of this when you wake up. I'd rather leave this town than read the bestiary for the umpteenth time.", Stiles murmured and gazed at the blonde girl with a severe expression. Stiles knew that was a lie however, he would never leave Beacon Hills and he would never remain out of supernatural mysteries. Bestiary, he thought to himself. Maybe the Argents would know something about the silver eyes. Stiles went for his phone again and wrote a text to Allison, detailing what occurred and what they observed. Hours and hours passed by and Stiles felt his eyelids becoming tired again. His body slid farther into the little chair and before he could fall asleep, the door opened with a loud bang. Stiles was startled in his seat and turned to find Scott standing in the doorway. He inhaled deeply and walked a few steps more so he could seal the door behind him. Scott's face looked anxious and his shoes and pants were coated in muck.

"What the fuck happened to you?", Stiles said with wide eyes and attempted to interpret Scott's emotions but he failed.

CHAPTER 2

Derek was missing. He didn't phone or contact anybody and Scott and Isaac couldn't trace his smell anywhere. Scott broke into Derek's Loft that night when he didn't answer any phone or text but he couldn't discover anything. All of Derek's possessions were still there, everything appeared normal. Just, that Derek was not there. After Scott informed Stiles of what occurred, he left the hospital again to look for Derek with Isaac. Stiles remained at the hospital, and even while his dread and anxieties caused his body to produce adrenaline, he fell asleep at some point.

With the pale light of the dawn, Stiles jolted awake to an abrupt noise. A faint rustling and a low sigh permeated the still chamber. Before Stiles's eyes could get acclimated to the bright light, he quickly leaped from his seat and hurried to the bed in which Selena was slowly waking. Stiles held her hand gingerly and hoped that it would calm her down, instead of frightening her.

"Hey, Selena. You're secure here. Maybe you remember me from the Eichen House. I'm..."

"Stiles.", Selena stopped his whispered words with a faint voice and turned her head towards him. Her eyes were still closed and Stiles was wondering, whether they were still silver.

"I'll just go and get a doctor.", Stiles murmured and tried not to exhibit any worry or bewilderment. Without waiting for a response, he drew his hand back and took a step backward to exit the room. Before he could turn back, Selena suddenly yelled out loud and sat upright in her bed. She moved so swiftly that it appeared as if a thunderbolt had struck her. Her silver eyes were wide open when she gazed at the wall and Stiles imagined that she shouted louder than Lydia did. Stiles's body froze in shock but shortly after, his worry changed into adrenaline and he was able to finally respond. He walked to the hospital bed and held Selena's hand delicately, he put his other hand on her face to move her head so she would look at him.

"It's alright, we can assist you. Nobody knows you're here. You're safe here.", Stiles replied with a loud voice to make sure she would hear him above her screaming. Her horror-filled eyes met Stiles's brown ones and she instantly stopped yelling. She gazed at Stiles like her life was dependent on it.

"Everything will be alright.", Stiles murmured calmly and focused on Selena's breathing which was finally going back to normal. Selena nodded her head so delicately that it was hardly perceptible, she closed her eyes for a second and opened them again, only to gaze at Stiles with light blue eyes.

"Are you in pain?", Stiles said and let his fingers fall from her face. Selena tightened her grasp around Stiles' fingers, Stiles tried to ignore the agony he felt and simply let her hold his hand. Selena's lips twitched like she was about to say something, but opted not to and merely nodded her head no.

"Are you hungry? I can grab you some water and a bagel." Selena didn't answer and simply continued gazing at Stiles. She seemed like she was lost in her thoughts and didn't find a way out of it. Stiles could see how torn she was, torn between the choice of whether she could trust him or not. Stiles was confident that the girl should drink and eat something, so he didn't wait any longer and attempted to pull his hand away.

"Please, don't leave. I-i...", Selena said and her voice was trembling. She was terrified, extremely scared. Stiles didn't sure whether he should ask her what she was terrified of or if he should simply stay silent. He chose to stay silent and merely nodded his head. With his free hand, he reached for the chair behind him and dragged it towards him so he could sit down. Selena maintained her attention on Stiles and for a few minutes, they simply remained quiet. Stiles could sense how Selena relaxed a little more with every passing minute. He was convinced that she felt okay again so he grabbed his phone and contacted Scott to meet him at the hospital with Deaton. Stiles hoped, that they would be there soon.

"Stiles?" Stiles was buried in his thoughts until Selena's words drew him back to reality. He lifted his head and looked at Selena.

"Did I lose my mind entirely or do werewolves exist?", Selena said and moved her head to the side to stare into Stiles' brown eyes. Stiles felt that it was sort of hilarious that this was her first inquiry and his lips twitched slightly.

"You did not lose your mind.", Stiles said honestly and watched how Selena's eyes weren't filled with so much dread now. If Stiles had learned one thing in the previous few years, then it was that the truth was the most essential thing. Every time they attempted to keep anything a secret, things only became worse. That didn't mean, that he would wander about Beacon Hills and inform every passing human about werewolves, banshees, and kitsunes.

"Do you want to tell me what happened?", Stiles questioned cautiously and stared at Selena with interested eyes. Selena thought about it for a few seconds before she eventually nodded her head and her grasp on Stiles' palm tightened again.

"I had a meltdown again three days ago. They kept me and gave me sedatives till I lay motionless. I suppose that they gave me too much or some inappropriate medication. I was in agony for days, experienced muscular cramps and my body felt like my veins pumped fire instead of blood. I slept there for three days till the night I ran away. Some guy came into my room that night, his eyes were burning red. And suddenly his face altered, his teeth, his hands, his legs, everything. He looked like a crazy wolf except that he was standing on two legs. He tried to choke me and then the last thing I remember is how I put my hands around his wrists and he suddenly froze. I fled away after that." Selena attempted to recall every moment but her recollections were foggy and she wasn't even sure, if all of this actually occurred, or if she simply lost her mind. At this point, Selena didn't trust herself or her recollections. Stiles thought, that he should say something to make her feel better, to let her know that she could trust him, to let her know, that she was secure. But he wasn't able to find the correct phrases.

"I know someone who will be able to assist you. They should be here soon, you don't have to be worried."

"They?", Selena said uneasily and Stiles observed that his words sounded like he would bring a complete team of physicians and therapists.

"My closest buddy, Scott. And his supervisor, Dr. Deaton. He's a vet. And my dad, he's the sheriff. He will make sure that the Eichen House won't come to grab you.", Stiles stated and observed how Selena widened her eyes.

"A vet? I don't know who's crazier. Me, believing I saw a werewolf or you, thinking a vet might assist me...", Selena whispered and stared at Stiles like he was insane. Stiles tried not to chuckle but felt his lips twitching slightly.

"Seems like it had a purpose why we met each other at the Eichen House." Stiles allowed his lips to form a grin as Selena laughed, but a few seconds later they heard a knock on the door. Sheriff Stilinski, Scott, Allison, and Dr. Deaton entered the room. Stiles could hear his tummy grumble as he spotted the bag of bagels in his dad's hands.

"Hello Selena, my name is Alan Deaton. That's Scott, Allison, and Sheriff Stilinski. We would want to assist you if that's good with you." Stiles believed that Dr. Deaton was one of the most compassionate and sympathetic individuals he had encountered. Selena shifted her attention to the people in front of her to stare at Stiles. Stiles only nodded with an encouraging grin to which Selena nodded and gently sat up in her bed.

"I would want to examine your heart, lungs, and blood first. It's nothing too horrible, I swear.", Deaton stated kindly and Selena nodded her head again. Deaton and Stiles both observed as Selena's gaze darted around the room anxiously.

"Hey, is it fine when I go and grab something to eat with Scott and Allison? My dad is the finest sheriff in the world, he will make sure that you're that secure.", Stiles stated and attempted to seek a solution where not too many people would be in the room when Deaton looked on Selena, but where he could also have the chance to tell Scott what happened to Selena. Everyone was silent as they waited for Selena to speak but she simply glanced at Stiles with wide eyes. She appeared to ponder about his notion but didn't seem to be persuaded by it.

"I'll come back immediately after that, I promise." Stiles' commitment was all Selena needed to nod her head yes again. While the three buddies exited the room, the sheriff gave the bag of bagels to Stiles and stroked his shoulder gently. Stiles merely grinned and reached for a bagel as soon as the door closed behind them. Allison and Scott didn't say anything and just let Stiles eat his bagel while they walked through the bright hospital hall. After Stiles swallowed his last mouthful, Scott couldn't suppress his interest longer.

"Did she tell you what happened?", Scott said and Stiles merely nodded but didn't say anything. Scott regarded that as a positive indication and waited patiently for Stiles to deliver them the tale once they entered the cafeteria. Stiles grabbed himself another breakfast and a coffee, while Allison and Scott merely sat down with him. Between the bites of his pancakes, Stiles finally related the account of what Selena had told him. Allison and Scott didn't say anything, they both appeared to ponder what Stiles just had stated and attempted to find any answer.

"Is there anything new with Derek?", Stiles questioned, after eating his last pancake and setting his dish away. Scott shook his head no.

"Isaac and Lydia want to seek for him today and maybe get Danny to trace his phone."

"Did your dad know anything about the silver eyes? Or could you locate anything in the bestiary?", Stiles questioned Allison but even Allison shook her head no.

"He has never seen a wolf with silver eyes and hasn't heard about it either. I didn't find anything yet in the bestiary." Again, Stiles just nodded quietly and nobody knew what to do or what to say.

"So, an alpha was there and attempted to murder her?", Scott said and tried to remember the full event again.

"Seems so. But why though? She didn't even know that werewolves exist till then. And I'm very sure that she doesn't even realize, that she's a magical creature or that her eyes sparkle silver. She didn't know anything about the supernatural until that night." Scott shrugged his shoulders and squinted his eyes, not being able to figure out what truly happened to Selena.

"Well, I don't know. But don't you think it's weird that some alpha shows up in town and suddenly Derek goes missing?", Stiles asked and looked at his friends with raised eyebrows.

"Well, there's no chance that this is a coincidence. There are no coincidences in this town.", Allison replied firmly, and with that, she conveyed the notion that ran through everyone's mind.

CHAPTER 3

Before the group left the café, Stiles bought a donut and some cookies, and a drink for Selena. He didn't quite know, what cuisine she liked or disliked, but he figured that every individual liked donuts and chocolate cookies. Allison knocked on the door and waited a second before she cautiously opened it. The three of them entered the room and glanced at Deaton with interested eyes.

"Selena looks to be completely fine. I shall analyze her blood at the clinic. Call me if she's in agony or anything.", was all Deaton said, as he said goodbye and left the hospital.

"I bought you some breakfast.", Stiles remarked and handed Selena the bottle of water and the food. Selena thanked him silently and set the meal on her lap while she had already taken a cookie.

"Dad, what happens to her when she gets discharged from the hospital?", Stiles asked his father who shrugged his shoulders with a concerned expression on his face.

"We will think of something, but don't worry, you will not go back to the Eichen House." Selena nodded her head while munching another cookie. The sheriff bid goodbye to the teenagers and left the hospital to go to work.

"I think we should discuss.", Scott continued as Stiles' dad left the room and looked at Selena. Scott seemed anxious and scared at the same moment. He knew he had to tell Selena the truth but he wasn't sure of how she would react.

"We will explain everything and maybe you can explain to us a few things too. You can trust us." Selena swallowed the remainder of her cookie and nodded again, and suddenly everyone was quiet. Nobody knew where to start and everyone was terrified of Selena's reaction.

"Stiles informed us what happened to you. Did you know the guy?", Scott inquired and folded his arms across his chest. Selena opened her mouth slightly, she looked like she was ready to say something but then decided not to.

"Why does anyone think that it's strange or weird that I claimed, I saw a werewolf? Why the hell is nobody screaming out or looking at me like I'm crazy?" Her question was extremely well founded. Stiles pushed his lips together, keeping himself back from telling her each and everything about the supernatural, thinking that Scott should be the one telling her. He was the alpha, thus he got the chores to do.

"Ok, listen, I... I will show you something. Just... don't stress out. And don't be afraid, I won't damage you or anyone, I promise." Stiles couldn't tell who was more nervous. Scott or Selena. Selena was nervous, she tightened her hands and gazed at Scott with wide eyes, terrified to miss something. Scott closed his eyes and was concentrating on shifting carefully and under control, so he would not shock Selena. He lifted his head again and opened his eyes. He glanced at Selena with burning, red eyes and showed Selena his teeth and claws from a safe distance. Selena didn't utter a word but the pals could notice how her breathing got deeper and how her eyes filled with fear. She moved back on her bed as far as possible and clenched her eyes shut.

"Hey, it's ok. Scott won't hurt you.", Stiles said and took a step forward. Selena tried to calm down and took a deep breath before opening her eyes again. She moved her head from side to side like she was struggling with herself believing what she saw. After that, she sat back in her bed and took a sip of her water.

"Just... tell me everything please.", she eventually muttered and stared at Scott with desperate eyes. She knew that whatever they would tell her, would change her life. But she also understood that she could not escape from the truth. Scott told Selena his story. He told her about Peter, Derek, and his bite, Allison and her family, and then Isaac and Dr. Deaton, and even a little bit about Lydia and Kira.

"What about you? Are you a werewolf?", Selena said and stared at Stiles who shook his head no.

"I'm just Stiles.", was all he said with a smile and placed his hands in his pockets.

"So, were you in the Eichen House because all of your buddies are some otherworldly creatures? I could truly understand if you say yes.", Selena whispered and Stiles thought it was funny. Even Scott and Allison pushed their lips together to hide their grin.

"I genuinely was possessed by an evil fox but no explanations needed, we got rid of this thing and I'm myself again.", Stiles said and Selena stared at him like he was either crazy or an awful comic.

"Are there any human beings left in Beacon Hills? What additional species are running through our streets?" Allison decided to tell her about Jackson, about the Oni, and to tell her more about Lydia as a Banshee and Kira the Kitsune. Selena's expression changed now and then. Her face changed from astonished to shocked to captivated and back to shocked.

"Alright, so Beacon Hills is plagued by all kinds of weird beings. And I was nearly slain by a werewolf. An alpha. How do I fit in all of this?" Selena narrowed her eyes while she processed all she had just been informed and thought about everything that had occurred to her. And even though she trusted those three strangers' every word, she could not find any meaning in it.

"We don't know, but we would like to find out.", Allison remarked as Scott abruptly cleared his throat.

"Selena, we truly think, that you are also supernatural," Scott answered cautiously and tried to retain her gaze, even though he wanted to look anywhere else but Selena's eyes.

"Why would you think that?", Selena said and Stiles could detect a mixture of fear and rage in her voice. Scott's eyes traveled around the room uneasily and stopped when he stared eyes with his best friend. Of course, the big evil alpha was too soft to communicate the awful news. Stiles rolled his eyes and saw Scott shrug his shoulders slightly.

"Your eyes. They gleamed silver when we found you."

"So you assume that I am a werewolf?" Selena asked and let her eyes drift between Stiles and Scott.

"No, werewolves don't have silver eyes. And I can't scent you. Not as a wolf or at all, to be honest.", Scott said and hoped that Selena would comprehend everything. And she did, but she loathed the idea, that none of this actually benefited her. All of those stories were not a remedy for her problem and she hated it, that she was a mystery.
“So what the hell am I”

Around noon there was a knock on the door and Misses McCall entered the room, to look after Selena.

"There are some guests.", she informed and Lydia and Isaac followed her inside the room. Lydia glanced at Selena with a bright and loving grin, before introducing herself and Isaac. Isaac kept a safe distance and stood next to Allison while crossing his arms over his chest.

"There's a doctor on the way to look after you, Selena. I suppose that they will let you go home today. I hope there's a plan yet, where she will stay?" Melissa gazed at her kid while asking the question, but didn't get the answer she hoped for. There wasn't a plan yet. Not even close.

"You may live at mine if you like.", Lydia remarked and glanced at Selena with a warm grin. Before Selena could speak, Scott turned her suggestion down.

"I'm sorry to say this Lydia, but an Alpha came after her to kill her. If he would show up again, you two are not secure."

"Oh no. Scott, no. Isaac is already with us, I don't have enough money to feed another magical teenager. I'm sorry, Selena.", Melissa said when she realized that everybody was looking at her. Scott sighed and suddenly everyone's gaze laid on Allison. Stiles thought, that Allison's residence should be safe enough.

"Oh! Yeah, yeah. I mean, I need to ask my dad but that should be ok, I guess.", Allison answered nervously and flashed Selena a faint smile. It was the greatest plan the pals could get at that moment so they just left it there. Just in time, the doctor entered the room to check on Selena.

"Did you hear something from Derek?", Allison questioned after they all left the room to allow Selena some peace while the doctor checked on her. Isaac promptly shook his head no.

"Danny could not locate his phone. But Lydia had an idea..." His voice went quieter at the end of the statement until it was only a whisper anymore. He looked at Lydia carefully who was already biting her lower lip nervously.

"I thought that maybe... Peter could help us.", Lydia said and looked at her friends with an innocent smile. Stiles could hear Scott growling and he didn't even have to look at his best pals to know, that his eyes were flaming crimson from fury.

"Scott, maybe it's not the worst idea. He knows Derek better than any of us do and he also understands a lot of stuff about the supernatural. Maybe he knows something about Selena. We should give it a try.", Allison replied and Lydia agreed. Even Stiles thought, that Allison was right and that Peter was their greatest chance right now. Stiles didn't like Peter, nobody did. But he understood more about werewolves, supernatural things, and Derek than they all did together.

"Fine. Try to call him or something and tell him to meet us at the animal clinic. And we will all go, nobody will talk to him alone.", Scott gave in and Lydia agreed before leaving the hospital to call Peter. After a while, the doctor, Melissa, and Selena left the room and greeted the friends in the hallway. Misses McCall was able to get Selena a frock and a set of shoes from the lost-and-found office. The dark blue dress reached down to her knees and the shoes seemed to be a bit too small but Selena didn't look like it would bother her. Selena was holding Stiles' jacket in her hands, which she used as a comforter the night before. She stepped up to him sheepishly and stretched out for him to give the jacket back to him.

"You may keep it till we get you your jacket.", Stiles smiled and put his hands in his pockets. Selena thanked him calmly and put the jacket over her shoulders and arms without thinking twice.

"Maybe we could go shopping while the boys talk to Peter." They all turned around to see Lydia, who was heading up to them and putting her phone back in her pocket. It seemed like Peter agreed to meet them. Stiles assumed that Lydia only looked for a cause, so she didn't have to see Peter but she also would never miss the chance to style a lovely female.

"Sounds good to me. Are you up for it, Selena?", Allison agreed happily and looked at Selena.

Selena didn't seem too excited and cleared her throat.

"I... I don't have money for it.", she muttered and moved from one foot to the other anxiously.

"Don't worry about that, sweetheart. If everything gets back to normal, we will get you a job or just sue the Eichen House for compensation. Until then, I will pay.", Lydia said and stretched her hand out for Selena to accept it. Selena looked at Stiles who smiled at her encouragement so she took Lydia's hand and left the hospital with her and Allison. Isaac, Scott, and Stiles drove to the animal clinic where Deaton was already waiting for them. Before he told them about what he found out, he went to the front door to replace the sign to closed, when an unexpected guest shocked him. Maybe Scott should have told him about their intention with asking Peter.

"Peter. What are you doing here?", the buddies could hear Deaton remark and did not overhear his hate.

"The true alpha invited me. Seems like he needs me." Stiles rolled his eyes and Scott growled again, thinking of what a stupid idea this was. Still, he found himself telling Peter about Derek and Selena only a bit later.

"Silver eyes? That's all? There are a dozen such supernatural beings with silver eyes.", Peter stated with an angry voice and folded his arms over his chest.

"There's actually something. Her blood is similar to Scotts. Like a werewolf.", Deaton stated and pointed at the little tube with Selena's blood in it.

"But she is not a werewolf. I'm sure of it.", Scott stated and narrowed his eyebrows while considering.

"You must have noticed something. Come on Scott, you're an alpha. There must be something. A scent, a shadow, a light, anything.", Peter replied threateningly and came up to Scott who looked at him with angry eyes.

"Her strength. She's stronger than a werewolf.", Isaac suddenly declared and everyone looked at him. Peter tilted his head and looked at Isaac who shrugged his shoulders.

"You mentioned that she was able to escape from the alpha. How could she do that without any help? She did not disclose anyone who was in the room with them. It was her and the alpha and she was able to get away from him.", Isaac explained and Stiles wondered when Isaac actually got smart and helpful.

"She said that she grabbed his wrists and that he kind of froze for a moment.", Stiles repeated her words and stared at Deaton.

"Maybe a venom? Like the kanima? Or some petrifaction thing like Medusa?" And that was the point where Stiles thought that he was wrong and that Isaac was, as always, not really helpful. Isaac merely shrugged his shoulders again and didn't seem to care that everyone looked at him like he was insane.

"Or like he lost his power.", Deaton murmured and exchanged looks with Peter who suddenly seemed uneasy.

"That can't be real.", Peter murmured gently but remained to look at Deaton.

"Her blood is not similar to Scotts because she's a werewolf but because she derives from werewolves."

"How can she stem from werewolves but not be one?", Stiles inquire and uncertainty pierced his voice.

"Lupus index potentate.", Deaton stated and looked at Peter who seemed to have the same thought.

"Could you translate that, please? Lydia is not here.", Stiles asked angrily and Deaton shook his head.

"Judge of the wolf might. I read about it once, there are some stories and legends but I never considered that they exactly exist. Werewolves usually recognize them by the name..."

"Goddess of the moon.", Peter ended his sentence and growled

CHAPTER 4

Isaac phoned Mr. Argent and informed him about Deaton's suspicion and hoped that maybe, he might discover anything about it in the bestiary.

"So, what do you know about the goddess of the moon?", Stiles inquired with wonder in his voice.

"Legends believe that a moon goddess holds the power of the moon. As you know, werewolves are sort of tied by the moon. So a moon goddess has the ability to govern the werewolves, she can take their power away.", Peter stated and still stood there with his arms crossed over his chest.

"You claimed, that she derives from werewolves. How can wolves have a successor that may be their deadliest enemy?", Scott remarked and stared at Deaton with uncertainty on his face.

"Well, according to the traditions and legends, a god or goddess of the moon, is the first kid in a pack, who is born without the wolf gene. The tales claim that the kid is so envious and furious, that it usurps the moon's power to take the power of another wolf.", Deaton continued as Peter eventually let his arms fall and cocked his head while gazing at Scott with angry eyes.

"Well then, let's take three guesses about who is responsible for Derek's disappearance.", he added as Scott took a step closer.

"You won't do anything until we know what truly occurred! I vow if you would come near her..."

"Then what? Do you honestly think I would simply sit there and risk that she will steal my power? And instead of defending her, you should start to worry about yourself since she probably won't hesitate to take a real alpha's power.", Peter remarked with a loud voice to which Scott changed into a wolf in one second and howled at Peter fiercely. Peter responded as swiftly as he could and fled the clinic. Scott transformed back to human and sighed.

"Great. Now there's not only an alpha pursuing Selena but also maniac Hale himself.", Stiles murmured and sat on Deaton's desk with a tiny jump.

"Text Lydia and tell them to come back here right now. Peter is probably ready to murder her.", Scott muttered and Stiles agreed, pulling his phone out of his pocket to text Lydia. Just after he pushed the send button, Isaac's phone vibrated.

"Mr. Argent discovered something. Here.", Isaac remarked and passed his phone to Deaton who glanced at the photo of the book.

"That's intriguing...", he murmured and continued reading. Stiles drummed his fingers on the desk uncomfortably as Scott stared at him with a furious frown.

"The stories are not true. Gods of the moon are children who are born on the night of a lunar eclipse. They are servants of nature, which implies they do not exist to do ill but to prevent it. They have the obligation to take the power away from those, who use it for murder, agony, and atrocities. That's why they are also dubbed Judge of the wolf power.", Deaton stated and grabbed for Isaac to give him his phone back.

"So, werewolves like Peter, Kali, and Deucalion? If so, then gods of the moon do a darn terrible job.", Stiles mumbled and still could not find any logic in all they had found out.

"Well, Selena does not realize that she is a goddess of the moon. If no deity of the moon knows about their skills, then it's not a surprise." Isaac was correct with that yet for Stiles, it still didn't make any sense at all. There were still so many pieces remaining so he could finally get the puzzle done.

"So, you tell me that nature gives a newborn the superpower of the full century and then don't inform them? Doesn't make them recognize and utilize it? No changing at a full moon? That's rubbish. After all, a werewolf understands that he's a werewolf."

"Well, why not? Jackson didn't realize that he was a Kanima...", Scott added and again, Stiles assumed that he was correct.

"Because he slaughtered mankind. Selena is intended to rescue lives and achieve justice. Why should nature grant her such skills and then keep them from her?" Stiles moaned and buried his head in his hands. His brain was spinning and aching from all the pondering, the puzzles, and the lack of sleep, food, and water. He felt weary, hungry, and perhaps a bit furious.

"Stiles is correct. We are missing something here.", Deaton muttered and strolled across the room uncomfortably when suddenly, Stiles's stomach complained.

"Anyone wants pizza?", he inquired and leaped off the desk to get back on his feet. Three pairs of eager eyes turned to him which he took as a yes. Stiles fumbled for his keys when he exited the clinic. Stiles gazed at the sky and realized that it already starting to dawn. He toyed with his keys in his hands and let them fall to the ground when he abruptly halted in his tracks. Someone was standing close to his car and supported himself with one arm.

"Derek!", Stiles yelled and began to sprint towards him.

Derek was weak, he was harmed yet he did not recover. Stiles wrapped his arms over Derek's shoulders to stabilize him and guided him inside the clinic. Even though he was glad to see Derek alive, he was somewhat upset, because he wouldn't receive any pizza now.

"Scott!", Stiles yelled while pulling the door open with one hand. Scott got there in less than three seconds and assisted Stiles to get Derek inside.

"Derek, what happened?", Deaton inquired and began to check on Derek, after they got him to lay down on one of the treatment tables.

"I lost my ability.", Derek murmured and forced his eyes tight as Deaton stroked his wounds.

"You're not an alpha anymore?", Deaton said and gazed at Derek with both, bewildered and startled eyes. Derek didn't respond and shook his head no.

"No. He's not a werewolf anymore. I can't sense him or feel this connection anymore.", Scott stated and Stiles watched how everyone immediately looked to fear as Derek nodded his head. Stiles realized that, at this second, everyone had the same name in their thoughts. Selena. Stiles thought about what Peter had said only a few minutes before and he wasn't sure anymore which fables and legends he should believe.

"Derek, we need to take you to the hospital if you don't recover.", Scott remarked and glanced to Deaton to seek assistance. Dr. Deaton only nodded and realized that he wasn't able to aid Derek in this scenario. Derek was a person now. Derek nodded again and sat up slowly. He stared into Scott's eyes and opened his lips.

"It was...", he started weakly before he passed out and Scott had to grab him, so he would not fall face first on the ground.

"Seriously? SERIOUSLY? I already hate him as a human.", Stiles grumbled and couldn't believe that the big bad wolf was not able to keep his shit together for only one more second to tell them a name. Scott gazed at Stiles with an expression, that reminded him of the one his dad had when Stiles did something dumb. While Scott attempted to pick Derek up, Stiles rushed outside to collect the keys he had misplaced when he noticed Derek.

"Hurry up, Stiles!", Scott screamed and looked to have issues with restraining Derek.

"I'm sorry that I'm not able to see in the dark. I'd like to remind you once again, that I am HUMAN!", Stiles answered and did his best to locate the keys with the assistance of just the dim light of his phone. Scott rolled his eyes, shut them down, and opened them again only to glance at Stiles with burning crimson eyes.

"Four steps to the left.", Scott led his best buddy so Stiles was finally able to take up the keys and drive them to the hospital. Just like the previous time, Melissa was the first one to see them. Stiles was sure that he saw her rolling her eyes before she came up to them.

"What happened this time?", she said and stared at Derek who was still blacked out.

"We don't know. But he's not a werewolf anymore, he needs assistance.", Scott muttered and Melissa recognized that this was serious. She didn't spend any more time and got a doctor and other nurses to aid her.

"I'll call you.", she added as she followed the nurses with Derek and went into one of the rooms at the end of the corridor.

"Do you believe that Selena did this to him?",
Scott eventually said and stared at Stiles who
shrugged his shoulders.

"I'm not sure what to believe anymore.", he said
and followed Scott back to the parking lot. They
drove back to the animal clinic and were met by
Allison, Lydia, Selena, and a huge pizza. It was
not a secret that out of these four, it was the
pizza that made the lad's eyes glitter.

"Was Peter able to assist you?", Allison inquired
and glanced at Dr. Deaton, knowing that none
of the three hungry males would answer her
while there was pizza to eat.

"No, regrettably not. I'm extremely sorry.",
Deaton lied and Stiles glanced at Scott and
Isaac who both tried not to seem astonished.
They assumed that Deaton must have a strong
cause to lie so they all didn't say anything.
Maybe it was best not to inform Selena of their
idea about her being a moon goddess when
Derek truly lost his abilities. Allison only
nodded and averted her head as she noticed the
headlights of a vehicle outside.

"That's my dad. Selena can remain with me until we find a better option. See you all tomorrow?", Allison inquired and picked up several of the shopping bags which were on the floor.

"Yeah, we will sort things out.", Scott stated and looked at Selena comfortingly. Selena nodded and thanked him before she followed Allison and Lydia who were carrying so many shopping bags, that it was hard for them to move.

"Oh, here. I acquired my jacket now, so you can have this one back.", Selena recalled and slipped off the grey jacket, which was far too large for her. Selena smiled and gave the jacket to Stiles who simply smiled at her faintly. Selena appeared so innocent to him. So shy, sweet, and with her sparkling blue eyes and her dazzling blonde hair, she nearly looked like an angel. Was she truly able to take a werewolf's ability away? To fight and to injure them? And if so, why would she do that?

CHAPTER 5

Stiles reached his residence late in the evening. His father sat in the kitchen and read the newspaper from the morning while sipping at a glass of water. Stiles felt it was hilarious how his father often grumbled about not having enough time to read the newspaper in the morning, yet refused to get up earlier to do it. The two of them chatted for a time, without mentioning any strange entity. Stiles missed this occasionally. The normalcy and the easiness of everyday living. Stiles headed to his room and dropped on his bed so his body finally rested for a bit. But just for one second.

"Stiles!", he heard Scott's voice, which sounded dull through the glass separating them. Stiles placed his hands over his eyes and moaned. Two hours. Two hours and there was already another problem? He opened the window for his best buddy tiredly, Scott closed it once he got in.

"What's up?", Stiles said and couldn't disguise the tiredness and irritation in his voice.

"Something's wrong. I feel... something.", Scott said and looked truly extremely perplexed and desperate.

"What do you mean? Something? Do you feel it in your head? Your stomach? Maybe it's just flatulence.", Stiles replied and felt sort of offended. He loathed information that wasn't even information. Something. What was it meant to mean?

"No, guy. It's like another werewolf is near to me. Just that the emotion is a lot greater than normal, sort of menacing. Like I have to surrender."

"Like an alpha?", Stiles said and sat up again, his head suddenly functioning again. Scott shook his head.

"No. I'm not sure. Maybe that happened to Derek too, when he lost his strength." Stiles nodded. Could be conceivable. Derek needed to wake up soon and tell them what truly happened to him.

"Do you think it's Selena?", Stiles inquired and was astonished when Scott promptly shook his head no.

"I don't think so. If it was her, Isaac and I would have felt it earlier. I meant we spent a lot of time with her." Stiles nodded again. He walked back and forth as he sought to find a response. He would not be shocked if additional mysterious creatures were prowling about Beacon Hills. Stiles simply prayed that if there would be more, they would be arriving one after the other so they wouldn't have to answer 99 Problems at one time. Before Stiles could voice his ideas out loud, Scott's phone began ringing.

"Allison, what's up?", Scott said into his phone and wrinkled his eyebrows while glancing at the ground. While Allison talked, he glanced back up at Stiles with huge eyes.

"We're on our way.", he said and terminated the conversation.

"The alpha was at the Argent's home.", Scott stated and Stiles moaned again. Of course, another difficulty. Why not? Scott shoved Stiles out of his room.

"Dad, I'll be back in a moment!", he called from the stairs and hurried outside to his vehicle. Mostly because he was not in the mood to address this with his dad. Just a few minutes later, Stiles halted the vehicle in front of Allison's home. Scott immediately leaped out of the vehicle before it even stood still and hurried into the home. Stiles rushed after him, only to encounter Mr. Argent with a revolver in his hand, Allison with her bow, and a very shocked Selena. Scott was saying something and looked to be upset about something.

"Where is he?"

"He's gone. We struck him with one of Kate's rounds, however. He'll be dead in less than three days.", Mr. Argent responded and wiped some blood from his face.

"Was that the same one who assaulted you in the Eichen House?", Scott questioned Selena, who only shook her head.

"Well, we don't need to worry about him anymore. Go home and get some rest, guys.", Mr. Argent insured them again and gazed at them like a concerned dad. Probably because he was a nervous father. Stiles felt sort of calm and knew that the Argents were the right place for Selena. Allison and her dad had everything under control. Scott thanked Mr. Argent before the lads left the home again.

"Do you believe the sensation you experienced was due to the alpha?", Stiles questioned Scott when they climbed back into the vehicle.

"I'm not sure. The sensation disappeared soon after I arrived at your place. Derek has to wake up.", he muttered gently and tilted his head to the side to see outside the window. Stiles didn't say anything, he only prayed that if Derek would wake up, he truly could assist them. Everything felt more convoluted than before and he wasn't sure anymore whether Derek possessed the answers they needed.

Since the alpha attempted to assault Selena in the Argent's residence, four days have gone by. Stiles wasn't sure if he was genuinely dead, it was too simple. But till today, he didn't come up again and everyone appeared to relax. Derek still wasn't awake, but Misses McCall reported, that he was growing better day by day. Isaac had informed Scott that he too got an odd sensation that night. They still didn't know what exactly created the emotion. Whenever the pack was in school, Selena assisted Dr. Deaton at the animal clinic. He even paid her. The pack decided she shouldn't be alone but she also wasn't allowed to attend school without a teacher phoning the Eichen House. Stiles's physic lessons were canceled this day, so he left the school two hours sooner. His father was at work and Scott and the rest of the pack were still stuck at school, so he went to see Selena. The bell made an unpleasant sound as Stiles opened the door and went into the clinic.

"Stiles, glad to see you. What can I do for you?",
Deaton inquired when he put his head through
the door to check who entered the clinic. Stiles
followed him inside and saw Selena holding a
cat on the table so Deaton could check on it.

"Finally, someone who can assist you with the
cats.", Stiles remarked and smiled, when he
recalled Scott telling him, that animals didn't
seem to like him anymore. Deaton chuckled but
maintained his eyes on his tiny patient.

"Hey Selena, I thought we could go someplace
and have lunch if you like.", Stiles remarked
and placed his hands in his pocket. Selena
grinned and nodded.

"Yeah, I'd love to if Dr. Deaton doesn't need my
assistance anymore.", she said and glanced at
Dr. Deaton who grinned.

"I'll be OK, Scott will be here in a minute
anyhow." Selena nodded and patted the cat one
more time before letting her go. She grabbed
her jacket and put it on before she bid farewell
and left the clinic with Stiles.

"So, what do you want? Pizza? Burger? Mexican?", Stiles inquired when they both hopped into the vehicle.

"Well, maybe... we can go to your apartment and make something on our own?", she whispered gently and glanced at Stiles with a bashful face. Stiles hesitated for a bit and thought about how to tell that girl, that he would rather be an alpha werewolf than be a decent chef.

"It's only that I ate canteen meals for more than a year. I simply miss homemade cooking.", she stated and glanced at Stiles optimistically. How the heck could he say no to that?

"Okay but I tell you, once you ate my stuff, you probably want the canteen food back.", Stiles cautioned her but only garnered a giggle from her. Selena informed him that no cuisine ever could be worse than the one they received at the Eichen House and Stiles simply listened to her, delighted that she finally felt comfortable enough to communicate. After reaching Stiles's place, Selena decided she wanted spaghetti with tomato sauce for lunch. She attempted to offer Stiles some simple jobs but truly wanted to handle everything on her own. Not because she didn't trust Stiles to be a competent chef, but because she missed doing regular things.

"How do you know how to prepare a self-made tomato sauce?", Stiles inquired as he only observed the water boiling. Selena shrugged her shoulders and concentrated on chopping the veggies.

"It was my favorite cuisine when I was a youngster, so my mom taught me at some time. Her tomato sauce was the best, I swear.", she answered without looking at Stiles. Selena never mentioned her parents before, she didn't tell anything about herself before and Stiles started to get curious. He tried his best to keep his mouth shut, not wanting to scare her by asking personal questions. After they finished lunch and cleaned the kitchen, they headed upstairs to watch a movie in Stiles's room. Selena instructed Stiles to select the movie as she chose their meal. While Stiles began

Spiderman on Netflix, Selena sat on his bed hesitantly, her feet still touching the ground. Stiles sat on the other side of the bed, with his upper body leaning against the wall behind him. With every passing minute, Selena seemed to relax a bit more until her back also reached the wall behind her and her legs were crossed on Stiles's bed.

"Do you think there are people like Spiderman? I mean, if there are werewolves...", she abruptly said but maintained her focus on the TV in front of them. Stiles shrugged his shoulders and thought that her question was more than justified. Scott and Derek would have thought it was absurd.

"To be honest, I have no idea what kind of creatures are running around in this world. It wouldn't surprise me, however.", he remarked honestly and folded his arms behind his head. Selena nodded and appeared to ponder about something before turning her head to gaze at Stiles.

"What do you think am I?", she said and her blue eyes peered so deep into Stiles's brown ones, that he believed it was impossible to lie to her. He lied anyhow, assuming that she wasn't able to discern falsehoods as werewolves could. They still didn't inform her about their notion of her being a goddess of the moon. Deaton thought they should wait till Derek woke up, just to be on the safe side.

"I don't know. What would you want to be?", Stiles said and glanced at her with a little grin. Again, Selena shrugged her shoulders and broke their eye contact to look at the screen again.

"A human. A typical, healthy person. Only someone who won't spend years and years of their life in various homes, just to be locked up in a psychiatrist because they're some monster and don't even know it." Her remarks were coated in dark sarcasm but Stiles could detect the grief in her voice regardless. He saw how she breathed harder and how she blinked much too rapidly, trying to stop tears from flowing.

Stiles came closer to her and laid his palm over hers softly.

"Hey, you're not crazy. There's just a side inside of you, that you haven't got to know yet. But we will find out what it is, I swear. And anytime we will know, we will assist you to regulate it and live with it alright. I mean, it's a part of you and as long as if it's not a Nogitsune or Kanima, you should live with it."

"But what if it's a Nogitsune or Kanima, or maybe something worse?", Selena asked and still seemed worried.

"Well, then we shall rescue you. Like we rescued Jackson and like my buddies saved me. We never let anybody down." Selena smiled a bit and looked at her hands, just to avoid Stiles's gaze.

"I was fortunate then, that you were the one who discovered me.", she remarked and glanced back at Stiles with a smile.

"Very lucky. I mean aside from all the supernatural calamities surrounding us.", he said and grinned when Selena laughed.

"I don't mind. As long as I'm with you, I feel secure.", Selena murmured gently and twisted her hand around so she could connect their fingers. And for the first time in Stiles's life, he fell silent.

CHAPTER 6

Three days passed when Derek eventually woke up. He felt better. The type of better you may feel after becoming entirely human. Scott visited him to tell him about Selena and the alpha and hoped that Derek could tell him what truly happened to him. And he did. It was not Selena, who took Derek's strength. Derek was in the woods when an alpha ambushed him and grabbed it from him. Derek didn't know him, but when he described him to Scott, Scott was positive that it was the same alpha who attempted to murder Selena. The pack was delighted, that Derek was awake and that he was getting better, but he did not offer them the answers they hoped for. Selena and the alpha remained a mystery. Scott didn't inform Derek about their notion of Selena being a goddess of the moon, he believed it would be a good idea if they would first get to know one other. Maybe he was frightened that Derek might respond the same way his uncle did. On a Saturday morning, the entire pack assembled in the hospital to see Derek. Derek was already waiting for them as they entered the little room. He still didn't look very great.

"What's wrong?", Lydia muttered as she observed Selena glancing at Derek with a bewildered face. Selena glanced at him with narrowed eyes.

"No, nothing. I simply... got a hunch.", Selena said and averted her look.

"You mean, down there? Don't worry, every straight woman gets that emotion when they meet Derek for the first time.", Lydia replied and shrugged her shoulders, thinking that Derek looked much more desirable as a vulnerable human.

"What? No! I... gosh, no.", Selena whispered and stared at Lydia with a surprised expression on her face. Lydia returned the astonished expression, recognizing that Selena genuinely meant it.

"Oh my gosh. Sel, are you... lesbian? That's wonderful!"

"Oh fantastic, there are some lovely females at our school, we can...", Allison abruptly said when she and Kira shifted their attention to the girls' chat, believing it was much more intriguing than the lads talking about supernatural difficulties.

"Lydia, no! I am not lesbian.", Selena murmured, rolling her eyes at seeing Lydia's countenance altering again. She would not drop that issue.

"Wha-... what type of men do you prefer then if you don't find Derek Hale attractive?"

"Are you bi-sexual? We're okay with it, don't worry.", Kira entered their debate and Selena felt like banging her head against a wall. She was done with that issue.

"Oh my goodness, I like Stiles!", Selena shouted a bit too loud, and immediately the entire room became silent. Selena felt everyone watching her, she bent her head to the floor, covering her face behind her hands, and moaned. At that moment, she wanted that the alpha would rush through the door and murder her.

"Uhm... well that's Selena by the way. The lady I told you about.", Scott stated after clearing his throat, freeing Selena from the unpleasant situation. Selena stared at Derek for a brief period and waved at him, he reciprocated it by shaking his head one time.

"Do you know any shapeshifter with silver eyes? Anything that can aid us?", Deaton questioned Derek to which he only shook his head.

"No, but if silver eyes are the only thing you observed, you're far away from a solution. That's pretty much nothing. You must have a preconception already, otherwise, you wouldn't come here." Deaton looked like he felt caught, even though he knew that Derek knew the pack too well.

"Well, really there's one tale that came to my mind.", Dr. Deaton said and glanced at Selena, who suddenly appeared quite engaged in the subject. She went a few steps nearer to listen to them, abandoning her hiding location behind Lydia and Allison.

"Selena, you mentioned that the alpha attacked you and that you were able to flee because he froze for a brief while." Selena bowed her head and stared at Deaton, waiting for his response.

"So, there must be a reason for it and I believe that reason is the key. If nobody was inside the room with you, you must have been the cause for it. I mean, you probably did something to induce his freeze. And that's why I thought of the tale of the lupus iudex potestate.", Deaton stated and Selena did nothing but stand there with question marks within her thoughts.

"It means something like the judge of the wolf's strength.", Lydia interpreted, attempting to assist Selena to find any sense in all of these phrases.

"Indeed. Most people name their deity or goddess of the moon, however. Someone who can take away the power of a werewolf."

"What the heck are you talking about, will someone kindly tell me what it means?" Selena was frightened, her hands were shaking and her voice was wavering. Stiles wasn't sure whether it was fury or grief, but either way, he simply wanted to console her.

"We performed some research. The deity of the moon is a kid who was born by a werewolf on the night of a lunar eclipse. They receive their authority from nature, they are intended to administer justice. It's their role to seize the power of the ones who abuse it for chaos and evil." Deaton's voice was soothing but Selena couldn't seem to relax.

"This girl can be anything but she's certainly not a goddess of the moon.", Derek muttered all of a sudden and Deaton turned his attention to him.

"You know about the legends?" Derek nodded his head.

"Yeah, my mother informed us about them. Apparently among her group was a deity of the moon born when she was a youngster. But it's exceedingly doubtful that gods of the moon even exist anywhere. For generations, wolf offspring that are born on the night of a lunar eclipse be murdered not later than three days after their birth. We are talking about werewolves here and we all know those who use their talents to hurt others. So they murder the infants to prevent themselves."

"How do they discover them though? It's not like every pack had a mad uncle like yours.", Isaac replied and held his hands in defense when Derek flashed him a furious glance.

"That's reason two why she can't be one. They have a tremendously powerful aura, werewolves can sense it from miles away, thus it's simple for others to discover them. If Selena was a goddess of the moon, the two of you would undoubtedly know.", Derek stated and swapped eyes between Scott and Isaac.

"Wait a minute, we both got such a sense when the alpha was at the Argent's home. Maybe he's a god of the moon, I mean he also took your power, right? Who knows, maybe they don't have silver eyes, maybe they are simply regular werewolves with a particular ability.", Scott replied and everyone attempted to follow his ideas. It did make sense, however. Derek shrugged his shoulders.

"I don't know. My mom never informed us how they appear or whether they could change, no one probably ever lived long enough to find out about it." Again, the room went silent. Instead of obtaining answers, they simply received more questions and riddles and Selena began to feel agitated. She was angry. Not at Derek or Deaton, or Scott, but because of everything.

"Fine, so the already dead alpha was a deity of the moon. What the heck am I and what did he want from me?"

Selena was furious when she heard the lines "We will find out" and "We are missing something" multiple times and left the room without any other words. She understood that everyone tried their best to support her, but this didn't alter the reality, that this entire scenario was too much to cope with. Selena exited the hospital and slowed down her speed as the fresh air surrounded her body. The cold air made its way to her heavy lungs and she was finally able to breathe again. In the center of the parking lot, there was a bench, encircled by all the automobiles. Selena sat down and closed her eyes while taking long breaths. She sensed how someone was seated next to her but refused to open her eyes. And she didn't need to since she already knew who it was, simply by his warmth and aroma.

"I'm sorry, I didn't intend to be disrespectful.", Selena murmured and slowly opened her eyes, still not looking at him.

"It's alright, we understand.", Stiles said and Selena could feel his stare on her. Of everyone, Stiles tried the most. Or maybe she simply felt as he did. Every time she looked at him, Selena wondered how he was able to withstand all of that. This existence in this city, with continuously being at risk to save someone's life. And every time, she believed that Stiles was the strongest of all of them. It wasn't Scott or Lydia, nor Kira or Allison. It was Stiles, who remained himself, still human, while everything around him exploded into flames, drawing agony and death. And he was the only one she genuinely trusted. Whenever Selena was around him, she felt this funny sensation. It seemed like magnets attracting each other, a sensation of knowing she would be grabbed if she would fall. It was the same emotion she got when she saw Derek earlier.

"Do you want to leave?", Selena heard Stiles remark and eventually turned her head to look at him. She bowed her head and got up slowly. Stiles grinned faintly and sought for his keys, fiddling with them until they reached the vehicle.

"Where do you want to go?", he inquired with a smile as they both sat in the quiet automobile.

"I don't know.", Selena whispered and clenched her fists, so her fingers would stop moving around nervously. There was a chaos of messy thoughts inside her head and chaos of messy feelings inside her body. And she wasn't able to sort any of it, she didn't even know where to begin. All she wanted was peace. A place where she felt safe, where she could rest. Selena only wanted to go home, but she didn't have a house. So she thought of the one spot, which seemed near to the sensation of home.

"Can we go to your place?", Selena inquired and stared at Stiles, hoping he wouldn't ask any additional questions. His grin morphed into a warm smile, nodding his head as he started the vehicle. Stiles chatted the entire time, giving Selena tales of the pack, Lacrosse, or school. Selena merely listened and smiled, thinking about how the bond between Stiles and Scott probably functioned in the way. Stiles chatted and Scott listened.

"Oh, my dad is home.", Stiles noted as the vehicle parked in front of his house. Stiles leaped out of the vehicle, Selena slid out slowly and locked the door gently, frightened to damage anything. She followed Stiles into the home, seeing him pulling off his shoes and dropping the keys on the little table next to the entrance. His motions seemed like he was on autopilot and Selena thought about how much she missed such things. Entering a room and feeling so comfortable and safe, that your body just does its work on its own, no need to think or worry about anything. Just feeling home.

"Hey Dad!", Stiles yelled and headed into the kitchen, Selena following him. She shyly stood in the doorway and greeted the sheriff who sat at the kitchen table with a cup of coffee, a piece of cake, and a lot of papers in front of him.

"What are you doing here? I assumed you wanted to see Derek to address some supernatural difficulties." He inquired and took a drink of his coffee. Selena waited for Stiles to speak until she glanced at him and saw that he was busy devouring cake.

"I wanted a respite from the otherworldly troubles. Or maybe from all the troubles.", Selena said and turned her head again to gaze at the sheriff.

"That's understandable, you must be puzzled."

"No, I... I honestly believe I'm sort of upset.", Selena blurted without thinking and for the first time, she was being honest with herself. Anger was the one sensation she could properly identify, it was the only feeling that reminded her that she was still alive, that she was still human. Selena observed as Stiles and his dad exchanged glances before Stiles placed the cake down and grabbed her hand.

"Come.", he merely muttered and took her upstairs to his room.

"So, you're furious. I mean that's fine, just let it out as we learned at the Eichen House.", he replied and stepped in front of Selena. Selena recalled the numerous hours of therapy when she was meant to experience rage and learn how to cope with it. It was intended to help her let go of her anguish and thoughts but the fact is, she was never able to. Selena was never able to experience wrath since she replaced it with remorse.

"I can't.", she murmured and gazed at the wall behind Stiles. Stiles disregarded her remarks and took a couple of steps closer, pausing only a few inches away from her. He delicately grabbed her hands and put them on his chest.

"C'mon, push me.", Stiles pleaded and Selena shook her head no, still unwilling to look at him.

"Go." Stiles let his hands fall from hers and Selena rolled her eyes, knowing that he wouldn't stop until she would try. She groaned and pulled Stiles away from her weakly. Stiles retained his balance without any difficulty and didn't even shift his feet.

"Try again. Do what they instructed us this time." Stiles put her hands on his chest again. Selena sighed again, shutting her eyes. She attempted to gather all her ideas, anxieties, and sensations. She thought about the scene back in the hospital, the irritation, the desperation, the terror. She imagined how her memories turned into fire, took a deep breath, and pictured how the fire moved from her chest through her arms and how it escaped from her hands when she pushed Stiles again. Selena opened her eyes and watched that Stiles adjusted his foot to retain his balance.

"Good, but there's more." Selena put her hands on Stiles's chest and closed her eyes again. She felt as Stiles stiffened his muscles, making it much more difficult for her to shove him away. And again, she imagined the fire inside of her. But this time, she thought of everything, she recalled everything. And with every recollection, her pulse raced quicker and her breath got heavier. She could feel how the heat flowed through her veins, her body scorching as she clamped her eyes tight and pulled Stiles away from her. And suddenly, something changed. Selena felt rage in every part of her body, she felt how new air entered her lungs, searing as it left again, and how her heart beat the blood through her veins to every part of her body. She opened her eyes to discover Stiles standing in front of her. Everything felt brighter and she was able to catch every ray of sunlight. Stiles was encircled by a golden light, shimmering like the halo of an angel. Stiles took a step back but abruptly halted in his tracks.

"Keep going." So Selena did. She continued her moves until Stiles struck the wall with his back. Selena stood in front of Stiles and breathed deeply, her hands were still on his chest and her muscles were burning. Stiles simply stood there and gazed into her dazzling, silver eyes. Stiles softly gripped her wrists, her gaze following his motions. And soon Selena couldn't do anything but focused on the sensation of his hands stroking hers. She noticed how her heartbeat returned to a rhythm and how her muscles started to relax. Selena closed her eyes, opened them again, and observed that the dazzling light and the golden sheen were gone. Stiles exhaled out and put one hand at the back of her head, wrapping the other arm over Selena's shoulders to bring her closer. Selena leaned her head on his chest and placed her arms around his waist, holding his t-shirt for fear of Stiles ever letting her go again.

CHAPTER 7

Stiles didn't know how long they both stood like that, he simply tried not to move. He attempted to hug Selena and hoped, that it would assist her somehow. After a time he heard Selena breathe out and observed how she gently let go off him.

"Thank you.", Selena replied gently and raised her head to gaze at Stiles. She let her arms fall to her side and bowed her head again, a strand of hair falling into her face. She slipped it behind her ear and took a step aside when Stiles ultimately pulled his arms from her body.

"Are you feeling any better?", he said and sat on his bed, observing Selena who was still standing in the center of the room, lost in her thoughts. She bowed her head and glanced around the room.

"I simply want to know what I am. I don't care about the alpha or Derek. I know it's selfish but

I just... want to know who I am.", Selena said and glanced at Stiles.

"Sometimes, it's good to make yourself a priority. And we won't stop hunting for a solution till we will discover one, I vow. You simply need to be patient." Selena bowed her head and the room became quiet for a few seconds before Selena groaned. She massaged her eyes with her palms and Stiles believed that she looked like a blend of desperation, exhaustion, and helplessness.

"Maybe you simply need a day off. One day of normalcy."

"I don't even know what it is.", Selena giggled and let herself fall into Stiles' bed with another sigh. Her feet were still touching the ground as she lay on the bed, looking at the ceiling above her.

"Things like... going to the theater, watching a lacrosse match, going to a party and getting drunk, even if it's illegal.", Stiles thought out loud and grinned when he heard Selena giggle.

"Sometimes it just seems like I lost 2 years of my life you know. Before my parents perished in this fire, I had this type of normalcy. I had friends and activities. I went to prom and at the end of the night, I sobbed because my date kissed another lady. I spent the summer with my buddies at the lake, we attempted to acquire booze but failed horribly. I entered High School and my pals and I planned this wonderful school life and how we would go to college together after that. Our main anxieties were whether we'd split up with the attractive basketball player or if we'd attempt a long-distance romance.

But suddenly, I lost my parents and my home. I bounced from foster home to foster family, failed all of my grades, and lost interest in my interests and friends. And... I truly didn't want to live anymore. I didn't even try. At some point, my desires for this magnificent future transformed into regrets and the only want I had anymore was to quit living. So I tried it. I mean, I attempted to cease breathing, to stop living. I failed however and landed myself in the

Eichen House where I spent another year of existence. I mean, I got better though. I am better. Just, still more existing than living I think.

While relaying her tale, Selena lay there on Stiles' bed, looking at the ceiling with her hands on her tummy. She didn't look anxious, or bashful. She was calm and serene as she recounted Stiles her most terrible recollections. And although Stiles could hear his heart tear, her voice didn't crack once.

"Hey, I got an idea.", Stiles suddenly stated as Selena turned her head to look at him. Stiles didn't sure precisely how to respond to her remarks, but he sensed that pity or grief were not things Selena wanted to hear.

"We should write you a list. With all the things you need to catch up, like the regular adolescent stuff." Selena's lips transformed into a grin as she shifted her body so she would sit on Stiles's bed, her legs crossing. Stiles smiled and rose to fetch some paper and a pencil. He retrieved some items from his desk before he sat next to Selena again.

"You definitely need to go to one of Lydia's parties and ride Scott's motorcycle.", Stiles thought out loud when their options grew fewer. Selena nodded and became lost in ideas of what else she could have missed in the previous two years. Stiles did the same and toyed with the pencil in his hands while pondering.

"Have sex for the first time.", Selena whispered without any warning and Stiles startled, looked at Selena with huge eyes and let the pencil drop to the floor.

"Oh my gosh, you're behaving like I just begged you to take my virginity right here. We're not that distant, wait a few days." Selena murmured and grinned at Stiles, choking back her laughter. Stiles still didn't answer and his cheeks became crimson, Selena eventually giggling.

"I'm just kidding, Stiles. Now grab the blasted pencil and write it down." Stiles did what Selena instructed him to and eventually managed to not feel humiliated anymore. He placed it on the list anyhow, having sex for the first time being number 14 on the list.

"Ok, one last one. Maybe plan a large birthday party.", Selena added and watched Stiles jotting it down when he suddenly glanced up at her.

"Selena, what is your birthdate?", he inquired in a serious tone and rose to fetch his phone.

"19th November 1994.", Selena said and began to feel worried, she didn't like how Stiles suddenly turned all serious and looked to be strained.

"Why didn't we think of this sooner.", he grumbled and entered something into his phone, Selena stepped closer to him to see what he was searching for. Lunar eclipse 1994. Selena knew what Stiles was searching for and was even more scared. They both understood, that this would be the evidence for Selena being a goddess of the moon. Stiles clicked on some links, opened a website, and scrolled through it until they reached a list of November 1994. Selena was sad when her birthday was not mentioned in the list but she got a peculiar sensation when she realized that the night from the 17th to 18th of November was listed.

"One day before my birthday.", Selena whispered softly and observed how Stiles also peered at the calendar with narrowed eyes. They both believed, that this couldn't be a coincidence.

"What if my parents merely altered the date of all the paperwork to protect me? Maybe I wasn't born on the 19th. It would make sense, right?" Selena glanced up from the TV to look at Stiles who nodded his head.

"Could be a possibility. Where were you born? Maybe we may uncover any notes or paperwork regarding you or your mother at the hospital."

"Beacon Hills Memorial Hospital. We didn't live here but my mother worked there as a nurse before I was born.", Selena said and Stiles nodded, promptly ringing Scott's phone to ask him when his mum was working again. And Scott knew, he would have to beg his mum for illicit aid again.

Stiles and Selena spent the remainder of their day together until it was dark outside. Stiles volunteered to take Selena back to Allison's apartment, where Allison already waiting for her at the threshold.

"What are you doing outside?", Selena questioned and heard how Allison slammed the door behind them.

"Isaac just went home and sniffed Stiles, so I figured he must be carrying you home.", Allison said with a smile and started up the stairs, Selena following her.

"Oh, Isaac was here. I see.", Selena remarked playfully and twitched her eyebrows, even though she knew that Allison couldn't see her.

But even without seeing Allison's face, Selena knew that she rolled her eyes.

"And you spent the entire day with Stiles.", was all Allison said as she reached the floor, turning back to gaze at Selena with furrowed eyebrows. Selena averted her eyes uncomfortably and shrugged her shoulders, her cheeks flaming nevertheless. Allison merely chuckled and opened the door to her room.

"Hey, I know it's been a hard day for you. What do you think of a lady's night with Lydia and Kira? Just a usual sleepover, we eat sweets, watch some movie, chat about males." Selena smiled when Allison used the term normal and quickly thought of the list she prepared with Stiles. Selena chose not to tell Allison anything about her birthday and the moon eclipse and felt that ordinary sounded wonderful for one day.

"Yeah, I would love it. I'll just take a short shower.", Selena said excitedly and observed how Allison nodded her head with a grin. While Selena had a nice shower, Allison contacted

Lydia and Kira, inviting them both over for a sleepover. Selena had already felt so much better after the outpouring of wrath earlier and the chats with Stiles, but she felt like the hot water washed away the rest of her unpleasant emotions and thoughts. She really felt absolutely great for once when she walked out of the shower. She dried her body and hair with a towel and opted to wear grey sweatpants and a white, long-sleeved blouse, placing her damp hair into a bun. Allison and Selena prepared some snacks and beverages and arranged them on a little table close to the window. Before they both could reach for any food, Kira and Lydia had knocked at the door. Even on a regular lady's night, Lydia looked like a top model with her blue dress and her red high heels. But Selena didn't anticipate anything else and merely grinned while rushing upstairs again.

Allison and Lydia rested on Allison's bed while Selena and Kira sat on a carpet, their backs resting on the bed behind them. Selena had a bowl of popcorn in her palms, and Kira took one piece after another.

"So, let's speak about you and Stiles. Did anything happen today?", Lydia suddenly inquired with arched eyebrows and pushed a piece of chocolate into her lips. Selena tilted her head so she could gaze at Lydia.

"No, nothing occurred. What about you and Isaac though? We all know that a lot of things occurred already, when will you make it official?", Selena shifted the subject and glanced at Allison who shrugged her shoulders.

"I don't know, I suppose Isaac is still terrified of Scott."

"Oh come on. We all know that Scott likes Kira, there's no use in pretending anymore. Scott is over this.", Lydia muttered and rolled her eyes. Allison was just about to say something when a loud noise unexpectedly interrupted her. The females glanced at each other, holding their breaths without even recognizing it. Just a few seconds later, they heard another crash.

"Someone is below.", Allison muttered and stood up gently.

"Your dad?", Kira questioned anxiously and watched Allison shake her head. Her dad wouldn't be back until Monday.

"Come on.", Allison replied and tiptoed to her door, cautiously opening it. It was silent for a brief period until another huge smash filled the air. The four females winced and immediately spotted the alpha standing at the other end of the stairs.

"What the hell?!", Allison yelled and slammed the door.

"That won't stop him!", Lydia cried as everyone moved away from the door.

"I know! Call Isaac and Scott!" Allison reached under her bed and brought out her bow and arrows. While Lydia attempted to phone Isaac, Selena continued walking backward until her back touched the wall. Kira still stood in front of the door, pulling off her belt and suddenly holding a blade in her hands. Selena didn't sure whether she was dreaming or truly gone insane but she was pleased nevertheless. Not barely a second passed before the alpha stepped inside Allison's chamber. Selena began to fear, seeing it was the same alpha that has attempted to murder her twice. Allison fired the first arrow and struck the alpha. He lurched backward and drew the arrow out of his chest. Kira attempted to aid Allison to battle the alpha, striking him with the sword but became sidetracked when they heard Scott's voice. The alpha utilized the moment of confusion and pulled Kira to the side, her head striking the floor. Allison fired another arrow, the alpha already catching it in the air and letting it fall to the floor. Allison stepped backward, knowing she didn't have enough time to launch another arrow. The alpha grabbed Allison by her neck and pressed her against the wall, making it impossible for her to breathe. Scott entered the room, his eyes burning crimson as he assaulted the alpha. Allison slumped to the ground, gasping for oxygen. While Scott attempted to battle the alpha, Selena went towards Allison and Lydia aided Kira. Selena didn't know how, but the alpha seemed even stronger than the last times and it didn't take long until Scott was held in the same trap as Allison. Selena noticed how her fear turned into anger and she thought back to the situation with Stiles. She closed her eyes and attempted to absorb all of her rages, turning them into flames. Selene opened her eyes again, knowing they shined silver. Allison's astonished face confirmed her.

"Leave my friends alone, I know you want me.", Selena suddenly shouted loudly and stood up, addressing the alpha. He let Scott go and took a step forward. Through her improved sight, she was able to record his motions incredibly quickly and before his hands could even touch her, Selena seized his wrists. She peered into his crimson eyes and felt some type of excitement going through her veins. The alpha halted and didn't move anymore, his face slowly began to shift, a human face becoming evident. But when the energy reached Selena's heart, she suddenly felt pain. Like the fire and energy had turned into poison.

Selenas eyesight went fuzzy and all she could see anymore was blackness and blood. For fear and anguish, she let go off the alpha and sank to her knees. It took her a few seconds before she was back to awake. She raised her head and found that the alpha was gone.

"Selena, are you ok?", she heard Kira exclaim and felt two arms around her torso, lifting her up. Her gaze went over the room and she exhaled deeply, pleased that everyone was fine.

"What the hell? I thought he was dead?!", Scott suddenly yelled and transformed back to his normal self.

"We all thought that. How did you know he was here? I didn't get to call you.", Lydia wondered and finally stood up from the floor, helping Allison.

"I was in the animal clinic when I felt this sensation again. I still feel it, it's powerful.", he said before the room fell silent for a few minutes, everyone attempting to digest what just had transpired.

"Stiles is on his way, I can hear the jeep.", Scott replied and peered outside the window, going downstairs without more comment. The girls followed him outside, just before Stiles and Isaac leaped out of the vehicle.

"What happened?", Stiles questioned and locked the door of his car.

"The alpha was here again. I felt this emotion again and promptly came here. Did you feel it, Isaac?" Isaac nodded his head and crossed his arms over his chest.

"Yeah, already before Lydia called me but it faded soon after."

"How is that possible? I still felt that like two minutes ago.", Scott questioned and stared at Isaac with narrowed eyes, Isaac merely arched his eyebrows and shrugged his shoulders.

"Wait for a second, everyone be quiet.", Lydia suddenly said and raised her hands in the air, begging everyone to hush talking. She pinched her eyes tight and appeared to ponder about something before opening them again, glancing at Stiles. "It's Stiles."

CHAPTER 8

"W-what do you mean?! Simply because I was possessed by the Nogitsune, it doesn't mean I am every monster now, just because we can't locate the actual one!", Stiles argued and was truly startled that Lydia even thought about it.

"Of course not, foolish.", Lydia responded and rolled her eyes. She straightened her clothing and took a step forward.

"I suppose that it's not the alpha that produces this emotion Scott and Isaac have, it's Selena. And because of it, the alpha can track her every time. And I guess, that the reason, why you both don't feel it anymore, is Stiles.", Lydia attempted to express her ideas, but simply stared into puzzled faces. She rolled her eyes again and moaned, bored of being the wisest of them.

"Ok now, listen. Since the two of you discovered Selena, she and Stiles saw each other every day. And I suppose that Selena sort of borrowed his fragrance to protect herself. Like, she's not conscious of it clearly, but I guess her inner wolf or goddess of the moon or whatever, utilizes Stiles's smell to cover up hers. I mean, most of the time they are together anyhow and when he's not near her, her body and clothing still smell like him. I assume today and the first time, the alpha could only follow her since his smell was not on her anymore. You took a shower straight after arriving at Allison's place and donned fresh new clothing, exactly like last time." The pack was finally able to follow Lydia's ideas and for the first time, something truly made sense. And their idea about Selena being a moon goddess undoubtedly had been true the entire time.

"So that implies that Selena simply needs to smell like Stiles to be safe? Move in with him and don't take showers anymore, troubles solved.", Isaac replied and shrugged his shoulders. He was so sensitive.

"Yes, that does assist us a lot but that's not the answer, stupid.", Lydia remarked again and stared at Isaac with an irritated face.

"Okay fine, it helps us to keep the alpha away from her, but can we finally speak about what Selena just did? Am I the only one who fully freaks out because of it?", Kira eventually remarked and glanced at their pals with large eyes. Stiles didn't know what Kira was talking about and saw how his pulse sped up.

"What do you mean?", Isaac said and took a step closer, now displaying more curiosity.

Allison recounted what just had transpired and how Selena usurped the alpha's power for a brief while. Scott added that he didn't have any more qualms about Selena being a moon goddess and his pals couldn't do anything but agree.

"If Selena's a goddess of the moon, then what is the alpha? He can't be a typical werewolf if he took Derek's power.", Isaac reasoned and presented another difficulty.

"I don't know. Okay, listen. Stiles and Selena will go to the hospital tomorrow to learn about her birth date. If you're already there, go and see Derek and tell him everything. Isaac and I will chat to Deaton again and Allison, maybe you can offer Lydia and Kira a section of the bestiary to discover anything that defines the alpha.", Scott remarked and everyone nodded in accord. It was a truth that Scott was born to be an alpha and Stiles believed, that his closest buddy did a terrific job. The ladies agreed it would be preferable to remain at Lydia's home till Mr. Argent would be back in town so Allison and Selena went back inside to gather a few things together. Isaac, Stiles, and Lydia waited for them as Scott took Kira home on his motorbike. After a short while, the ladies found themselves walking up the driveway to Lydia's home, happy that Stiles volunteered to accompany them there.

"Selena, wait!", Stiles yelled and staggered out of the vehicle, chasing after her. Selena turned back and paused as Allison and Lydia walked inside. Stiles halted in front of the blonde girl and took off his jacket, giving it over to her.

"If all of this is true, then you're at least safe with that.", he replied and watched her accepting his jacket with a grin.

"Thank you, Stiles.", she replied in reply and slipped a strand of light hair behind her ear. Stiles only smiled and Selena turned around to enter the home. She waved at him before locking the door behind her, hiding in a, presumably, safe dwelling.

"Wow, you like her.", Isaac observed as Stiles hopped back into his vehicle, rolling his eyes.

"Can't you simply walk back to Scott's house? Or at least shut up for once?", Stiles replied in answer and started the vehicle. Isaac laughed.

"That's precisely what Derek would say to you.", Isaac remarked chuckling and Stiles couldn't do anything but agree.

"Selena.", someone muttered and Selena brought her knees to her tummy, forcing her eyes tight to go back to her pleasant dream.

"Selena, wake up." Selena moaned and slowly opened her eyes, her cheeks becoming bright crimson as she noticed Stiles standing over her. Mostly because she was hugging with his jacket, as a tiny child would snuggle with their favorite soft toy.

"I'm sorry. Lydia and Allison went to Allisons to grab the bestiary and didn't want to wake you up. I didn't want to wake you up either, but Scott's mom is in the hospital for just two more hours, so...", Stiles babbled uncomfortably and took a step back, making some room for Selena to rise up.

"It's alright, they could have awakened me up.", Selena mumbled as wiped the sleep out of her eyes.

"I'll wait downstairs.", Stiles merely responded with a tiny grin and exited the room. Selena looked for clothing in her bag and put on black trousers and a beige sweater that Allison had given her. It was too long for Selena so she merely placed the end of the sweater into her trousers. She combed her blonde hair and placed it into a ponytail, racing to the bathroom incredibly fast to wash her face and brush her teeth. After a few minutes, she headed downstairs, meeting Stiles in the corridor. Without further comment, she unlocked the front door and strode outdoors, Stiles following her.

"How are you feeling?", Stiles questioned as Selena put the seatbelt on.

"I don't know. I simply want to know the truth.", Selena said and shrugged her shoulders, not sure how to react after all that had transpired. Stiles bowed his head and concentrated on the road. He was silent and Selena felt like something was odd.

"Are you ok? You seem exhausted.", she murmured when she had looked at him really for the first time this morning. She hadn't noticed his pale complexion and the blue circles beneath his eyes before. Stiles twisted his head to glance at Selena for a second, before glancing back at the road.

"I don't sleep that well every time I find myself in a supernatural tragedy.", he added and grinned faintly. Selena recognized the emotion. Since she left the hospital, she didn't sleep more than 4 hours a night. Sometimes, she felt like losing her mind but her body kept going anyhow. Probably knowing, that she didn't have any other alternative. They both remained silent, everyone immersed in their own thoughts until Stiles stopped the jeep in front of the hospital. Selena followed Stiles into the hospital and soon noticed Misses McCall at the registration desk. She observed them and directed them to follow her into an empty room.

"These are the only things I could uncover on you in our system. I didn't discover anything about your mother, but 18 years ago, everything was kept in writing form. So, I shall inadvertently lose this key card now, which can unlock the door to the document archive of the gynecology department.", Misses McCall stated and gave Stiles some papers and a key card. Stiles snatched it and placed it into his pocket.

"Thank you very much for your assistance, Misses McCall.", Selena remarked nicely and noticed how Misses McCall nodded her head with a loving grin. Stiles and Selena exited the room following Misses McCall and made their way to the elevator, heading to the 4th level. They followed the indications and discovered the document repository soon after. Stiles peered in every direction a few times before unlocking the door with the key card. They entered the room gently and closed the door without any noise. Selena exhaled in relief and located a light switch, making the room bright. There were 4 enormous shelves, all loaded with dozens of boxes.

"Okay, let's go.", Stiles muttered and began peering into the boxes. Selena opted to start at the opposite end of the room, discovering a shelf with patient files shortly after. She sought the box with the names beginning with W and pulled it out after finding it. She opened the dusty box and glanced through the files with her finger. Winchester, Williams, Winderwood. Wilson would have been between those files. Selena glanced over every name again and moaned as she knew, that she wouldn't find her mom's name in it.

"The file of my mom is not here.", Selena remarked loudly, making sure that Stiles would hear her. She placed everything back into the box and put it back onto the shelf.

"Here are some files arranged by dates. Maybe we can locate the file of November 1994.", Stiles said as Selena made her way over to Stiles, helping him to discover the proper box.

"Here we go.", she heard Stiles remark after a while and observed him setting the box down on the floor. She got closer to Stiles and bent over him to get a peek at the files he opened. He opened the file for the month of November and browsed through the pages until he reached the page with the date 19th November 1994.

"There was not even one birth on this day. And your mother wasn't here on this day either."

"Look at the days before that.", Selena urged and watched Stiles flip the pages. He studied the papers attentively, without saying anything for a long.

"On the 18th November, a lady entered into labor at 00.34 am. It was the sole birth at this day.", he read and Selena could see how abruptly, his entire face became pale.

"What? Was that my mum?", Selena said anxiously and had to stop herself from tearing the file out of Stiles's hands. Stiles merely shook his head no.

"No. The paperwork states it was Talia Hale."

"Great, so some Talia Hale gave birth to a kid on 18th November. That's not helping us.", Selena remarked and folded her arms over her chest. Stiles gazed up at her with an expression that Selena hadn't seen on him before.

"Talia Hale is Dereks mother. And Derek only had one sister and she was older than him.", he said slowly and looked at Selena like he had just told her, that her favorite dog had died.

"Stiles, what the heck are you trying to say?", Selena finally replied and already knew what his response would be. She didn't want to hear it however, her mind and body both fought to disregard the truth.

"Selena, I suppose the reason why you never realized your mother was a werewolf is because she was not a werewolf. And the reason why her name doesn't show up in any records is, because she never gave birth to a kid." Stiles remarked gently and looked at Selena attentively. Selena merely remained there, replaying his words within her brain over and over again, until finally recognizing it.

"You assume that Talia Hale is my mother."

CHAPTER 9

Stiles pulled the paper out of the file, folded it, and placed it into his pockets where he previously stored Selena's patient file. He closed the file and placed it back inside the box, rising and pushing the box into the shelf.

"Come on, we need to speak to Derek.", he murmured and softly grasped Selena's hand. Stiles pulled her behind him and opened the door with his free hand. He made sure that nobody was in the corridor and immediately slipped out of the room, shutting the door gently once Selena had followed him outside. Since Stiles informed Selena of his notion about Talia Hale being her mother, she hadn't spoken a word. He wasn't sure whether she was upset at him, or maybe simply astonished, but either way, he didn't have the time to worry about it right now. He realized they had to speak to Derek to ultimately find out the truth. Stiles let go off Selena's hand, as they both stood inside the elevator. It was peaceful until Stiles heard Selena shift. He looked around and noticed how

Selena's body was shivering. Selena had her eyes closed and continued walking backward, hoping for anything to cling onto. Her breathing was heavy and uneven as she slammed the metal wall with her back.

"Stiles, I can't breathe.", she muttered uneasily while her hands clenched into fists, her knuckles growing white. Stiles understood the sensation just too well.

"Hey, it's alright.", Stiles remarked and went closer to Selena, reaching out for her hand. He encompassed her left hand with both of his hands, observing how stiff her body was.

"I will assist you to open your hand now and when I do so, you will breathe out, ok? When I'll aid you to shut it again, you will breathe in. And so forth. Ok?" Selena nodded her head and opened her eyes. Her blue eyes were filled with terror as she observed Stiles's hands opening hers and she pushed herself to breathe out, just like Stiles did. She exhaled out, till her hand laid flat in Stiles's grasp. When she felt how Stiles moved her fingers back into a fist, she inhaled in. They both did the technique a few times and Selena managed to calm down. She had her eyes closed again, beginning to feel peaceful with Stiles holding her hand and experiencing her breathing.

"Stiles, I...", she started but was stopped by the elevator door opening. She promptly opened her eyes and let her hand fall to her side, already missing the warm contact of Stiles's hands. Selena didn't utter another thing and got out of the elevator, Stiles following her.

"Hey, maybe we should get some breakfast before we speak to Derek. You didn't eat or drink anything yet and the entire situa...", Stiles began to remark as he observed how pale Selena was. Of course, she wasn't OK and she wouldn't be fine for long, but Stiles was anxious.

"I'm good, let's leave.", Selena stopped him and began to walk through the corridor. She paused in front of Derek's door and banged on it when Stiles finally reached her. Selena opened the door when she heard some of Derek's mumbling and Stiles gasped out loudly. Derek was upset with everyone, and Scott sent Stiles to speak to him.

"Hey Derek, how are you feeling?", Stiles inquired and moved next to Selena who crossed her arms over her chest to stop herself from moving about anxiously.

"Great. Did you discover something?" Wow, Derek was an expert at small conversation. Selena turned to Stiles and held out her hand, Stiles knew she wanted the documents. He dug for the papers within his pockets and gave her the document they had discovered a few minutes earlier. While Selena narrated to Derek the complete narrative of the alpha and her, Stiles studied the documents of Selena's treatment file when he suddenly discovered something. Selena was transported to the hospital two times because of mental breakdowns, two additional breakdowns were documented from the Eichen House.

"...so we came here to...", Stiles heard Selena remark and raised his head.

"Derek, when was the fire?", he interrupted Selena and could feel her gaze on him. Derek gazed at Stiles with an expression that Stiles couldn't figure out. It was something between death desires and uncertainty.

"15th February in 2005.", he said and Stiles matched the date with the one in Selena's file.

"Do you know anything about these dates? 3rd March 2011 and 11th May 2011?", Stiles inquired again and could see how Derek's perplexity became deeper.

"Yeah, on 3rd March, Peter murdered my sister and, on the 11th May, I killed Peter. Or at least, I believed I did." The concept of Talia being Selena's mother had simply been speculation thus far, but now Stiles was confident that Selena had some type of link to the Hales.

"Here, look. There are four mental breakdowns mentioned in Selena's file. Three of them on the dates I just questioned you about and the final one on the day that you went missing." Stiles gave Derek the paper and watched him read it. Derek raised his head again and shrugged his shoulders.

"So, this girl suffers a mental breakdown every time someone in my family dies? Well, you may be grateful then, because you're still alive.", Derek merely stated and stared at Selena coldly. Selena didn't say anything and gave him the other page.

"I was born at this hospital on the 19th November 1994. But hey, there was not even one birth on this day. On the 18th of November however, on the night of a lunar eclipse, there was one.", Selena added and peered at Derek with huge eyes, not wanting to miss any of his reactions. Derek read the article, then put it down and glanced at Selena, then looked at Stiles.

"Call Scott and tell him to meet us at his apartment. Now.", Derek stated firmly and gazed at Stiles.

"Now?", Stiles said bewildered as Derek's face steadily morphed into a furious one.

"Yes, Stiles. Right now.", Derek said and immediately took off every single cord and plaster from his body. Stiles simply stood there, not knowing what to do as Derek slipped on his pants and t-shirt and Selena gave him his jacket and shoes like it was the most natural thing in the world. Like Derek wasn't human and needed to remain in the hospital for at least four more days. And so, Stiles simply did what Derek instructed him to.

Selena sat in the backseat and observed as Stiles' fingers anxiously tapped on the driving wheel. She wasn't quite sure whether he was concerned about Derek sitting next to him, or about what they had just found out. But she didn't really care, she just wanted to lay her hand on his and comfort him, just as he had comforted her in the elevator. Selena loved Stiles a lot, but she was concerned that with all the supernatural turmoil, it was not the perfect moment to tell him. Or perhaps the appropriate moment to fall in love.

They went to Derek's apartment where Derek got out of the vehicle and returned back with a circular box in his hands a few minutes later. He didn't say anything and Selena resented it. She was part of all this too and he didn't tell them one word of his plan. When they approached Scott's home, his mother answered the door for them. Derek and Stiles welcomed her with a short greeting and promptly walked into the living room, while Selena halted in the hallway and attempted to sort her thoughts. She had never been to Scott's place before and she felt it was unusual that they gathered here to discuss otherworldly things. Not because it was Scott's residence, but because his mother was there. She was human and Selena believed that they should keep things like that far away from her. To keep her secure. But then she recalled, that Stiles was also human and he chose to be part of the magical realm.

"Are you alright with being part of this world?", Selena suddenly questioned and was just as astonished as Melissa. Melissa lifted her eyebrows and smiled warmly.

"I don't really have a choice, do I? My kid is a werewolf and I'm his mother.", Melissa responded and observed how Selena's look transformed. She looked sort of hurt so Melissa grabbed Selena's hands in hers.

"But you see, Scott is a good one. I am terrified of all those supernatural abilities but Scott, Lydia, and Kira, they all utilize their talents to serve others and make our world a little bit better. So does Derek and I'm sure you will too. This pack is terrific and I couldn't be any prouder."

"Do you think I can be a member of this pack someday?", Selena questioned nervously and Melissa chuckled.

"Sweetie, you already are a member of this pack and they will never desert you."

"Thank you, Misses McCall.", Selena responded gently and her heart felt warm. She missed talking to her mother like way, but chatting to Melissa felt almost the same. Melissa nodded and let go off Selena's hands, guiding her to the living room. Scott was pacing across the room uncomfortably, Derek and Isaac sat on the sofa and observed him. Stiles leaned against the wall next to the entrance, his arms folded across his chest. Selena felt her heart leap a bit and disregarded her inner voice begging her to go up to him and embrace him. She went over to him nevertheless and stood next to him, observing the other three lads.

"I've done this just once. And I did it with my claws, not with the claws of your dead mother.", Scott grumbled and looked at Derek.

"Scott, you already did it once and it worked. Last time, you were even able to pull out a dark kitsune out of Stiles fine, this time you only need to give me back my memories. And I absolutely won't ask Peter, don't even think about that possibility.", Derek stated calmly and glanced at Scott the entire time, his eyes following him as he still couldn't manage to remain in one spot.

"Okay, I will do it.", Scott eventually responded and sat near Derek. Derek retrieved the package he had received from his apartment and opened it. He placed it back on the table and flipped it around, something little dropping onto the table. It looked like claws. Derek put them back into the box one by one and then held Scott's wrist, holding his hand over the box.

"Wait, wait! What are you doing?" Selena interrupted them and walked up to them. Scott looked uncomfortable and she didn't want anyone to get hurt.

"Those are the claws of my mother. Alpha werewolves can impact our thoughts and memories with them. They can view our memories and also remove them from us, making us forget things. Scott used the same strategy to rescue Stiles from the Nogitsune. And with the claws of my mother, he can probably give me back the memories that she took from me. Depending on how long we can hold on, we maybe can talk to her.", Derek explained slowly and Selena was glad that he finally talked to her about his plan.

"What do you mean withholding on?", She asked and noticed how everyone exchanged looks.

"It can be dangerous and there's a chance of not coming back. But I trust Scott and if he's able to get us inside my mind, he will also be able to bring us back." Selena nodded and understood how important it was that Scott did what Derek asked him to. Derek's mother was probably the only one who could tell them the truth.

"Wait, us?", Selena inquired and Derek nodded. He didn't say anything and concentrated on Scott again. It appeared evident to Derek that Selena would be haunting his thoughts along with Scott and he didn't seem too frightened about it. On the contrary, Selena did feel terrified. Probably because she never thought that something like this was possible and also because she was scared of being stuck in Derek's mind forever. What if Scott wouldn't be able to bring her back? But Selena didn't have a choice if she wanted to get to know the truth and she believed Scott. And Derek.

Selena only nodded and took a step backward. Derek grabbed Scott's wrist again and positioned his hand just above the claws. Without any hesitation, he put Scott's hand into the box and Scott yelled out in agony, his eyes going crimson. It took him a few seconds to come back to his senses and rose, motioning Selena to the seat next to Derek. She did what Scott ordered her to do and observed Scott coming up behind them. Selena watched Isaac who walked up to Stiles, standing next to him. He seemed sort of concerned, much as Stiles did. Stiles forced himself to grin as Selena's eyes met his, attempting to encourage her, even though he felt more afraid than hopeful. But Selena smiled back at him, knowing that if Scott wouldn't be able to bring her back, Stiles definitely would be able to. Knowing that she closed her eyes and felt how Scott positioned his claws on her neck, suddenly feeling a sharp pain.

CHAPTER 10

Selena woke up in an abandoned home. It was dark and chilly, the walls and floor looked to be damaged and Selena saw evidence of a fire. She didn't recognize this area, but recalled that she was inside Derek's thoughts and was instantly confident that this had been Derek's house. Selena sat up from the chilly floor and glanced around.

"Derek? Scott?", Selena phoned and wasn't shocked, when nobody answered her. The only thing she could hear was the damaged wood beneath her feet, as she stepped to the door. She carefully opened it and felt the chilly breeze enveloping her. It was dark outside, but the moonlight allowed Selena to see the forests in front of her. Selena decided to seek Derek so she left the porch and gently headed into the forest. Suddenly the sky clouded as the moonlight disappeared, leaving Selena in full blackness. Selena paused in her tracks and she felt panic growing within her.

"Derek?!", she shouted again and whirled around, expecting to see anything. Anything. Suddenly there was a little noise, reminding Selena of wolves howling. The screaming became louder with every passing second and it soon evolved into a frightening snarling. Selena felt like an entire pack was around her, ready to murder her. She shut her eyes and told herself, that this was not real. Taking deep breaths, her dread progressively dissipated, until she unexpectedly heard a faint murmur.

"Selena." The roaring and snarling wolves were gone. Selena opened her eyes and realized, that the sky was clear again, the moonlight allowing her the opportunity to view the home and trees again. She turned around and saw a lady approaching her. The moonlight made her skin look pale, almost making her shimmer in the darkness. She approached closer and Selena was finally able to glimpse her face and black hair. The lady stopped just in front of Selena when suddenly a familiar voice said.

"Mum." Selena turned her sight from the lady to see Derek walking out of the trees. He glanced at Selena for a brief minute before he moved over to his mother to embrace her. The lady smiled and put a hand on his face as a proud mother does. Selena thought it was nice to see Derek like that. Like a tiny kid, yearning and needing affection from his mother, finally displaying feelings. He was not as cold-hearted as he pretended to be.

"You know me.", Selena abruptly stated and took a few steps closer. The dark-haired lady let her hand fall to her side again and turned her head to gaze at Selena.

"Yes, I am Talia. We knew each other when you were a tiny kid. You and Derek know each other as well, you will recall everything when you wake up. We don't have much time, however, so please let me explain everything." Talia didn't need any more explanations, she understood precisely why Derek and Selena came to speak to her. Selena felt like Talia had longed for this moment all along.

"I am very sorry that I had to remove your memories, but we had to do it to protect Selena.

I snatched the memories of every pack member, making them forget that I was pregnant. The only ones who knew that I was pregnant, were Lorraine Martin and your adoptive parents." While Selena maintained her focus on Talia, Derek continued gazing between his mother and Selena. He felt sort of anxious and Selena observed how it impacted her.

"Lorraine Martin knew that you would be born on the night of a lunar eclipse and I had to do everything to preserve your life. Joanna, your mother, was my midwife and she was not able to have children. She was also one of my closest friends and allies, and I knew she would be the only opportunity to keep you safe. She was not only a fantastic mother but also a witch. She tied your power with the one of our family, which means that as long as the power of the alpha would remain in our family, your power would be veiled. When Derek lost his power, yours emerged."

"My mother was a witch?", Selena said shocked and wanting to hear more about it, knowing, however, that there wasn't enough time to speak about everything.

"Yes, she was a servant of nature. Just as you are."

"Why did Selena have to go, while her power was hidden?", Derek said and took a step closer to his mother.

"Just look at her. Her beautiful blue eyes, her virtually white hair, and her pale complexion. It's the appearance of a goddess of the moon. It would have taken less than three weeks for other wolves to discover and kill her. Selena, listen to me. You have incredible abilities but it comes with a price. You can absorb the power of a werewolf, but you have to transmit it to another one. It's like magic. If it's there once, it can't be erased or destroyed. It's not your responsibility to simply accept it from someone. It's your obligation to preserve a balance, to make sure that the magic won't be exploited. As soon as you steal the strength of a wolf, another one needs to gain it."

"What happens, if I don't pass it on to another human?", Selena wondered and believed that she would never be able to transfer such abilities to any innocent person. Not, if they don't want it.

"If you would assemble the powers within of you, it will kill you." Talia grasped Selena's hands in hers and opened her lips like she was going to say something when suddenly they heard a voice reverberating across the trees.

"Derek! Selena!" It was Scott. Selena understood that he was there to bring them back to reality.

"That's all you need to know, you will remember everything else." Talia curled her lips into a modest grin and let Selena's hands fall to embrace Derek. She turned to Selena and put a palm on her face.

"I'm proud of the two of you. You two are a family now." Talia put a little kiss on Selena's forehead and then vanished into the trees. Selena watched after her, till Scott approached the two of them. Scott put a hand on Selena's shoulder and suddenly, everything went dark.

Selena felt like her entire body was lit on fire. Her skin burned and her brain felt like it was ready to burst. She shut her eyes and pressed her palms on her head, as all the memories came back into her mind. All the memories that Talia had stolen away from her, now played like a movie within her brain. There were Selena's mother and Talia, seated in the yard of Selena's old home. There was Talia, how she danced with Selena. There were recollections of herself, playing hide and seek with a boy and a girl. Selena recalled, how the dark-haired girl grasped her little hand and vowed to always protect her. She recalled, that the female's name was Laura, and the guy's name was Derek. She recalled, that the Hales had visited her every summer and that Talia had taken away their memories after every visit. Selena remembered everything. She knew Derek her entire life and she had known Laura and Talia.

Selena began to scream in agony, rising from the couch she was still seated on and trying to flee away. Her discomfort increased stronger and even with her eyes open, she couldn't see anything well.

"Selena! She's bleeding!" Selena felt two hands on her shoulders, making the anguish worse. She wrenched away and staggered backward, striking the wall with her back and shutting her eyes tight again.

"No! Go away!", Selena yelled as he felt someone grabbing her arms again.

"Selena, look at me." Scott's voice felt near and Selena managed to open her eyes, seeing the entire world in a golden glow. She recorded every tiny movement and could feel the anxiousness of Scott, Stiles, and Isaac. With the memories constantly coming back to her and her senses being overstrained, Selena felt like she was about to lose control at any second.

"Leave me alone!", Selena shrieked and Scott backed off, astonished by the fact, that her cries progressively changed into snarling. Selena attempted to take control of her body again, shutting her eyes to focus, but the anguish wouldn't leave. Her breathing grew erratic as her body felt like it was burning to the ground. Suddenly, Selena felt a hard hold on her shoulders, forcing her gently into the wall behind her. Before she could even lift her arms to resist the person, she felt the warmth of palms on her face. Her body absolutely froze, as she felt lips brushing hers, making her forget to breathe. Her thoughts fell quiet and her body appeared to chill down. When she couldn't feel the warmth on her lips any longer, she gently opened her eyes and peered into its brown eyes of Stiles.

"Stiles.", she muttered, before her legs gave way and everything went dark again.

CHAPTER 11

"Drink some water", Stiles replied and gave Derek a cup of water. The situation eventually began to quiet down. Selena had passed out and Scott had carried her to his room, where Melissa took care of her. Stiles was anxious but Scott informed him, that she simply needed some sleep and that she didn't feel any discomfort anymore. Derek had passed out shortly after they got back from his thoughts. He had just woken up and suffering from a terrible headache.

"What the fuck happened in there?", Isaac suddenly exclaimed and was courageous enough to speak out loud, what Scott and Stiles were both wonderings. Derek frowned at Isaac from his seat but set the cup of water down anyhow. He took a deep breath and told them what his mother had told him and Selena. Derek's speech was firm and calm but Stiles caught the break in his voice when he informed them, that Selena was his sister and that they had known each other their entire lives.

"Did she mention the alpha?", Isaac inquired, but Derek shook his head no. He put his fingers on his temples and massaged them gently, thinking it would make the headache go away.

"So, if Selena steals the strength of the alpha, she may give it back to you. And as soon, as you're an alpha again, her abilities will vanish again. That seems like the ideal answer to me.", Stiles concluded and put one of his fingers on his chin as he got lost in his thoughts.

"Yes, if she's able to do it. I don't know how to educate her to control it or to take the power at all. Or does any of you want to play the guinea pig?" Derek stared at Scott, then at Isaac but they both didn't respond. They both didn't want to risk the prospect of losing their abilities permanently, and Stiles could think of just one person who would genuinely deserve it.

"Peter." Stiles looked around to see who had stated his feelings and spotted Selena standing in the doorway. He felt the need of racing up to her, embrace her and then kiss her again, but something about her made his body stop. Selena looked irritated. Not furious enough for her eyes to shine, but angry enough to look more otherworldly than human. Stiles felt a deep hurt in his chest as he discovered, that she was averting his sight.

"Do you even know Peter? Don't you think he's well... too clever and too powerful to play the guinea pig for you? He will murder you before you can count to three.", Isaac stated and gently backed off, as Selena moved up to him.

"Just because you are terrified of him, doesn't imply that I am. He killed people. He murdered my sister. If I'm going to seize anyone's power, then it will be his. With or without you.", Selena growled and gazed at Isaac with furious eyes.

"And how precisely do you want us to achieve that? He's brilliant.", Scott remarked and was startled as Selena turned her head to his, her eyes instantly sparkling. Stiles didn't say anything, but he was convinced that at this moment, they were all more terrified of Selena, than they had ever been of Derek.

"Fool him, use wolfsbane, Kanima poison, or anything. I don't care, just do it."

"Selena...", Derek attempted but Selena shook her head.

"Lydia is picking me up, she's bringing me back to Allison. Just... do something about Peter.", was all she murmured before she exited the room. The lads gazed behind her and sighed, once they heard the front door slam shut. Selena wasn't herself and she reminded Stiles of Scott on his first night of the full moon. Something, he didn't want to endure again.

"What should we do now?", Scott questioned but gazed at three bewildered faces. Everyone realized that Selena's concept was based on vengeance and fury and that Peter was too clever for them to mislead him. But in the end, that was the only strategy they had. Just like that, Derek headed back to his apartment, thinking of a method to make Peter arrive there. Isaac, Scott, and Stiles traveled to the animal clinic to acquire wolfsbane and kanima venom. Right after the sun had faded, they all found themselves at Derek's loft with Peter in front of them, locked up and unable to move.

"That was far easy than anticipated.", Isaac replied and folded his arms across his chest, peering at Peter. Peter rolled his eyes and moaned.

"What the heck do you want?", he questioned and stared at his nephew who slumped against a table.

"Scott?", was all Derek murmured and gazed at the younger lad. Scott's eyes blazed crimson when his fingers morphed into sharp claws. Without any hesitation, Scott shoved his claws in Peters's neck, making Peters's eyes light blue. Scott showed him, everything they had seen in Derek's head, giving him back his memories. Peters's body recovered considerably quicker than Dereks and Selenas had.

"That's a friggin joke. A goddess of the moon. In our family?" Peter didn't appear astonished, he simply looked like he was fully done with his family. Or the entire globe.

"You being a werewolf is a fucking joke.", Selena murmured and came up to him.

"Selena, wait. We should think of something before you start...", Scott said but Selena had gone out for Peters's arms. Her grasp on his arms strengthened when her eyes transformed to a brilliant silver. The second Peters's eyes began to glow, Selena's muscles clenched and her face looked like she was in agony. The agony appeared to become worse, until she abruptly shouted and took a few steps backward, losing the grasp on Peters's arms. Stiles was going to approach her when he realized, that her legs and arms began trembling. Selena disregarded her body however and took a couple of steps closer to Peter again. She closed her eyes and inhaled deeply before clutching his arms again. Nothing changed however, with every passing second, she merely felt more misery. Selena didn't seem to care however, she continued attempting it again and again.

"Selena, stop it!" Derek instantly yelled and pushed her back by her shoulders. Selena swung back to him with wrath in her eyes.

"I have to learn it, right? I don't have a choice!"

"Yes, but not without knowing how. Let us assist you." Derek's voice sounded calm again, but Selena only shook her head.

"Nobody here has got any clue. You can't help me." With that, she made her way back to Peter, doing the same thing again and again. With every unsuccessful endeavor, she became angry, until the room was filled with hostility and retribution. There was nothing left that felt human, there were no feelings.

"She lost control.", Allison murmured and watched Selena lose herself.

"Maybe she needs an anchor.", Scott whispered and spotted Derek glancing at him.

"Scott, she's not a werewolf.", Derek informed him but Scott shook his head.

"Maybe she's more like us than we realize. She uses fury too. Without an anchor, no humanity. Without humanity, you can't judge reasonably. She won't make it, if vengeance and hatred are all she can think about, that's against nature. She needs humanity to make it." Derek realized what Scott was thinking and nodded.

"She will listen to an alpha howling then." Scott nodded slightly and closed his eyes to shift. He opened his crimson eyes and howled loudly. Stiles could feel the floor trembling and watched how Isaacs's eyes lit up golden. Selena turned around and glanced at Scott.

"Selena, you need an anchor to control it. Look for an anchor that will make you feel human again.", Scott replied and gazed directly into her silver eyes. Selena felt bewildered and went back to Peter.

"Oh my gosh, folks. She already has an anchor, just explain to her how to use it.", Allison replied and rolled her eyes, undoubtedly regretting not bringing Lydia and Kira with her.

"It's Stiles. Tell her to think about Stiles.", Allison stated as Scott nodded again, gaining Selena's attention again.

"Selena, think of Stiles.", Scott hissed and stared at Selena like it was an order.

"Selena, think of Stiles.", Selena heard Scott grumble, so she turned her head to him. She tried to fight against the immediate notion of Stiles in her head, but something in Scott's voice made her do what he commanded her to. Selena closed her eyes and thought about Stiles. She thought of the thrill she had, whenever Stiles had held her and how it felt to feel his heartbeat below her palms. She recalled, how every time he touched her, each cell of her body fixated exclusively on that portion of her body. And then, she recalled how he had kissed her, and instantly, her entire body froze. A feeling of melancholy overwhelmed her body, but it made her come back to reality. Back to humanity. For a minute, Selena thought about what she was doing and what she wanted to accomplish. She opened her eyes again and looked at Peter, tightening her grip on his arms. Selena could feel the pain rushing through her veins, but chose to concentrate on the sadness she still felt in her body. The anguish morphed into the sense of energy, that steadily made its way through her entire body. Selena saw Peters's face alter as if he suddenly felt agony and as his eyes stopped sparkling, Selena felt the energy in her chest. It was like an explosion, as she immediately felt the force in every part of her body. Her lungs felt like clouds were accumulating inside of them and it was hard to breathe.

"It worked.", Scott muttered and Selena observed, how everyone gazed at her. Selena understood that Peter did not deserve the power, but she would not give it to some innocent person on the streets either. So she closed her eyes again, putting her hands on Peters's chest, and focussed on the power within of her. She barely had the notion of giving him back his strength, when she felt the energy leaving her body again. Peter passed out and Selena felt weak. She stumbled backward into Derek's arms, who were fast enough to catch her. Selena let Derek hold her, as they were all watching Peter, waiting for anything to happen. Just a second later, he drew a big breath and opened his blazing blue eyes.

"Selena, are you ok?", Allison inquired and Selena could sense the fear in her voice. Selena shook her head no and pushed away from Derek's arms holding her up. She moved over to Allison who promptly grasped her hand. Nothing was fine. Maybe she was back to being human and maybe she had lost her wrath, but anger had been the only thing to keep her sane. Anger had been the only shield from all the anguish and uncertainty she would experience. Feeling human again, Selena felt lost. She felt lonely. She didn't know what she wanted or what she was meant to do. She longed to be with her brother, but at the same time, she didn't even know him. She wanted to feel powerful and be proud of her abilities, but at the same time, she simply wanted to be normal again. She wanted to kiss Stiles and find herself in his arms, but at the same time, she never wanted to look into his eyes again. She wanted to know about her original family, but at the same time, she didn't even know everything about the family that had reared her. And suddenly, all Selena wanted, was to be alone. To merely sleep and avoid reality, ideally forever.

"Take her back to your apartment.", Derek stated and glanced at Allison who simply nodded and led Selena outside. The two females didn't say anything till they reached Allison's home. Once they arrived there, the only words leaving Selena's lips were "I want to be alone" and Allison simply nodded again.

Five days passed by when Selena was alone. She stayed in her room and only spoke to Allison when they had supper together or when she brought Selena a new shirt of Stiles, so she wouldn't lose his fragrance. After five days, the door to her room opened and someone entered inside without any permission.

"Get dressed." Selena dropped the blanket that covered her, to see who stood in her chamber.

"Go home, Derek.", she whispered and heard him groan.

"Are you naked?", he said and Selena stared at him astonished.

"What?! No!"

"Good.", Derek muttered and ripped the cover off of her, leaving Selena in the cold.

"Now, get dressed and pack your suitcase.", he said and glanced at Selena, who simply curled up in her bed again, trying not to show Derek that she was truly chilly without the blanket.

"I'm not ready for more training. Just go home." Derek rolled his eyes and delved into the pocket of his leather jacket.

"I will and you are going with me.", he stated and gave Selena a piece of paper. Selena sat up in her bed and grabbed the paper, gently reading it. Guardianship of Derek Hale over Selena Wilson, née Hale. Selena read the words, again and again, slowly realizing that after all these years, she finally had a family again.

"Are... are you serious?", she muttered and gazed at Derek in bewilderment. Derek just nodded, but he couldn't hide the small smile on his lips. Selena jumped to her feet and ran towards Derek to hug him, not caring if he wanted the hug or not. Derek welcomed her embrace nonetheless, laying one of his hands on her head.

"So, you're going home then?", Selena heard Allison say and glanced to the doorway, where Allison stood with her arms crossed over her chest. She spent much too much time with Isaac. Allison helped Selena to pack her luggage, after that, Selena and Derek thanked Allison and her father for allowing Selena to stay with them. Selena and Allison have never seen Derek thus kindly. Just a few minutes later, Selena reached her new house.

CHAPTER 12

Derek climbed up the stairs, laying Selena's luggage down on the floor once he entered a room. Selena came into the room, her heart soaring in delight when she examined her new room. The walls were decorated turquoise, from above the bed, white drapes with fairy lights were dropping to the ground, making it appear like a canopy bed. Opposite the grey bed, three photographs of the ocean and the forest covered the wall. Right beneath them, two white easy chairs were put on a grey carpet. Underneath a huge window, a desk and a chair were put with a dresser next to it.

"Lydia arranged everything and Kira picked the furnishings. Scott, Stiles, and Isaac helped to paint the walls and everything.", Derek recounted and Selena smiled a bit, envisioning Lydia controlling everyone.

"I adore it. Thank you very much.", she said and took up the bags from the floor, walked towards the dresser to put her few items in it. Derek left her alone in the room and Selena attempted to take everything in as she set her items where she believed it was proper. She went downstairs slightly later and helped Derek to make some lunch. Selena had never envisioned Derek cooking or doing anything else regular and still felt a little bit strange around him. He was so self-contained that it was impossible for her to perceive him as a real person.

"Now that I live here officially, can I go back to school?", Selena inquired as they sat at the huge table together and ate the paste they had just baked. Derek stared at her with furrowed eyebrows and took a drink of water before speaking.

"You want to go back to school voluntarily?", he questioned and seemed sort of amused. Selena shook her shoulders, wondering herself whether it wasn't usual for magical beings to seek a regular existence. Did Derek even go to school? Probably not, she thought.

"Yeah, I mean I want to graduate and go to college. Or maybe not, who knows? But at least

I want a regular everyday existence, have the same possibilities as all other teens.", she continued and suddenly recalled the list she had prepared with Stiles. Thinking about Stiles, she quickly felt a stinging aching in her chest. Selena wasn't entirely sure what was worse. That she missed Stiles, or that she still felt upset over this kiss she couldn't even recall much. Which was the reason why she felt wounded in the first place.

"Fine, we'll go and register you then tomorrow.", Derek replied and Selena nodded trying herself to grin as she toyed with the fork in her hand.

"What's going on with you and Stiles? I thought you liked him.", Selena heard Derek remark and glanced up at him, looking like a young child who has just been caught with their hands in the cookie jar.

"I do.", she murmured and placed a noodle into her lips, pondering whether Derek was the best one to speak about Stiles to. Maybe one of the females would have been a better pick for that.

"Why are you ignoring him then?", Derek said and looked bewildered, putting down the fork.

"Because he kissed me."

"And... you didn't want that?", Derek inquired again, trying incredibly hard to find any sense in the words of the girl. He already felt overstrained at that moment and tried to recall what it was like to be a brother or what it was like when Laura tried to be a nice big sister.

"No. I mean, sure. Just... not like that. I mean, he simply did that to calm me down when I freaked out. Which worked by the way, but still. I can't even recall it properly and so I'll always believe that my first kiss with him was this pity kiss which I can't even remember. I just... I wanted him to kiss me because he loves me, not to avoid a panic attack.", Selena stated and watched how Derek nodded in understanding, apparently delighted that he was finally able to grasp her thoughts.

"Okay, see. Stiles is odd but I mean, he's a decent man and he truly loves you. I don't believe he tried to harm you, he only wants to assist and sometimes he just doesn't think before he does. So if you like him, just speak to him fine. I mean he is one of the few individuals here you can genuinely speak to and who listens." Derek whispered the last sentence, thinking of Isaac and Scott and suddenly felt happy that out of them, Selena selected Stiles. Stiles was obnoxious but he at least understood what he was doing. Selena nodded, knowing that Derek probably was right. She could either get up the courage to tell him how she felt, or she could keep walking around with that heavy feeling in her chest.

"Derek, can you take me to his house?"

Stiles had not been able to focus the entire day. Instead of concentrating on his studies, all he could do was thinking about Selena and wait impatiently for her to contact him back. Every time they gathered at Derek's apartment to have Selena's room done, Stiles wanted to see her there. Nothing occurred however and he was confronted with the realization, that she was ignoring him. Lydia attempted to convince him, that Selena also didn't text her or Kira, but it didn't make him feel any better. He had kissed her out of nowhere. Right at the moment, when she received her memories back. The timing could not have been worse and he understood, that she didn't want to see him now. Not that it would erase the reality, that he was wounded by it.

"Hey Stiles, can we talk? I may have uncovered something, that might assist us with the alpha.", Kira murmured and tore the kid out of his thoughts. The girl dumped a stack of paper on the table before sitting down. Kira, Lydia, and Allison had attempted to study the bestiary in the previous three days, hoping they would uncover something that would give them a competitive advantage against the alpha.

"What is it?", Stiles questioned, when he had sorted his thoughts and was able to focus on anything else.

"This one. It's a monster called Coraptor. It might steal a person's character, or like, their soul. They live but are not able to experience emotions anymore or to have like, a distinct character. It's like they sink into profound sadness.", Kira stated and shifted the page, so Stiles could see it.

"I mean, Derek does give me some unhappy emo kid feelings, but I don't believe that this is what happened to him.", Stiles said and glanced back at Kira, not comprehending her point.

"That's what I thought too, but then I got this notion. Like werewolves are both, right? Human and wolf. So in a sense, their character has two sides. Maybe even two souls? Maybe the Corpator stole his wolf's persona. Like, Derek lost his side of the wolf but preserved his humanity. According to the bestiary, the Coraptor borrows the character of a human to become a human itself. The more characters or humanity he takes, the more human he gets. What if the Coraptor concentrates on werewolves? Taking their wolf sides to become a werewolf itself. That would explain why he's closer to a wolf than a human. Because he takes the wolf sides solely. Instead of being human, he's becoming..."

"A second Peter.", Stiles whispered and Kira nodded, reminding him that this was precisely what she was thinking. Stiles thought, that everything of Kira's ideas was made logical. It would explain how the alpha could take the abilities, without murdering other alphas and how he's more animalistic than human.

"We should meet at the animal clinic with Scott and Deaton after school. Maybe we can think of something together.", Stiles suggested and Kira nodded. She retrieved the paper again and placed it on top of the stack before putting it back in her bag. Scott approached their table a few seconds later and sat next to Kira. Stiles and Kira didn't bother to explain their new notion again, both knowing that Scott had previously listened to them when he had collected his lunch from a few feet away.

"Do you believe that Selena would be able to steal the power of the alpha? If your idea about the Coraptor is accurate, then we don't know how much power he truly possesses. She already battled with Peter and he's not even an alpha.", Scott stated before stuffing a mouthful of fries into his mouth.

"I mean, we could murder him. But then, Selena would maintain her power and Derek wouldn't get his one back.", Kira said and shrugged her shoulders, thinking that they just had two possibilities here.

"Maybe she can practice it. She could try to take the powers of two wolves at the same time. Like a workout, so she can become stronger.", Stiles stated and used his fork to move his salad from one side to another on his plate.

"And who should be those werewolves? I doubt that Peter is going to volunteer.", Kira remarked to which Scott lifted his head to look at Stiles.

"Me and Isaac. She gave Peter his power back, she will do the same to us." Stiles nodded slowly when he observed that Scott was waiting for his approval. Scott simply was like that. He would always go through the flames for his buddies and he would never allow someone innocent to suffer because of their difficulties. Even if it meant he had to sacrifice himself.

"Did Allison contact you?", Stiles abruptly inquired and attempted to mask his impatience, knowing however that Scott could hear his pulse accelerate up. Allison had missed a few courses in the prior days, to take care of Selena. Kira and Scott shook their heads. The pair of them didn't say anything, however, knowing that any form of encouragement wouldn't be enough to cheer up the scared child.

"She texted me a few minutes ago.", Stiles suddenly heard a soft voice and glanced up to see Lydia. She put her purse on the table and sat down next to Stiles. Lydia observed his tense motions and rolled her eyes.

"Derek escorted her to the loft. She looked to be thrilled about it.", she stated and smiled softly. Scott and Kira reciprocated her grin, even Stiles felt better, knowing that Selena now had a proper home. Stiles spent the final few courses just as inattentive and anxious as before. He was relieved when he finally heard the bell ring for the last time that day. Just before he exited the building to meet Scott and Kira outside, he felt his phone vibrating. His hands rushed for his phone quicker than he could even think about it and his body froze, when he finally saw her name on the display. On my way to you where all the text messages stated. It was enough for him to lose his sanity.

"Scott, I must go! You and Kira have to meet Deaton on your own!", Stiles called over to his buddy who was waiting for Stiles in his car. Scott only grimaced and nodded, moving back exactly in time before Stiles could smash him with the vehicle.

CHAPTER 13

Selena paced up and down the porch uneasily. Her thoughts were racing and for a brief period, she thought about running away. She had never been adept at talking about her emotions and she did not have an idea where to start. Before she could reconsider her mind, she saw Stiles Jeep come into the driveway. Selena closed her eyes for a few seconds and opened them again when she heard the door of the vehicle slam shut. The girl observed as Stiles raced up to her and before her body could respond with any moves, she had found herself in a tight grip. And all of a sudden, all of her anxieties had been removed. Selena put her arms around his body and hoped for the moment to never end.

"Come on, let's go inside.", Stiles replied and broke the embrace. Selena wanted to sigh as she saw Stiles going up to the door and opening it. She followed him inside nevertheless and locked the door behind her cautiously. Stiles threw his bag next to his desk as he entered his room before he turned around to face Selena. While Stiles made care to put space between them, Selena finally realized how her thoughts had deceived her. She instantly realized, that her heart and her body knew the truth all along. Stiles did care for her. He liked her and he would always defend her. And everything she felt in his presence was not just because she liked him, but because he felt the same.

"I'm sorry that I kissed you out of the blue. It was selfish and I...", Stiles started to say uncomfortably and glanced at Selena with shame in his eyes.

"I'm not.", Selena interrupted him and came up to him before throwing her arms around his neck. Selena kissed him softly on his lips and kept her face close to his while waiting for his reply. Stiles put one hand on her hip to bring her closer to him and placed his other hand on her face before kissing her again.

"I'm sorry that I disregarded you.", Selena remarked after breaking the kiss. She let her arms fall from his neck, across his shoulders, and down to his chest to linger there for a time.

"You're already forgiven.", Stiles muttered and put his hands on her neck cautiously, his thumbs brushing her cheeks tenderly. Selena smiled faintly and closed her eyes as she felt his kisses on her face. Stiles let his right hand slip off her neck and where she had just felt the warmth of his touch, she instantly felt his lips. Her body responded far quicker than her mind could conceive, making Selena tilt her head back and burying her fingers in his shaggy hair as Stiles continued kissing her neck. Selena opened her eyes for a brief while and observed the pinboard behind Stiles. The list they both composed jointly grabbed her attention, making Selena grin. Selena let her hands fall from his hair and groped for his grey t-shirt. She made a step backward, making Stiles's lips lose the touch with her flesh. With a firm grasp on his t-shirt, Selena continued walking backward, making Stiles follow her until her legs met the wooden bed. Selena lay down carefully, thinking that she never felt anything greater than Stiles's warmth as he leaned over her. Stiles put his hands near to her head to stabilize himself but leaned down anyhow to kiss her again. He interrupted the kiss after a brief period and Selena felt the cold blanket her as he attempted to rise. Selena responded swiftly and grabbed his t-shirt again, pushing him back down on her.

"Stiles, I... do you recall number 14 on the list?", Selena whispered gently and saw as Stiles squinted his eyes while thinking. Selena grinned a bit as she waited for him to recall.

"Oh. Number 14.", he said and nodded gently before glancing back at her. Selena stroked her fingers through his hair again, until she abruptly halted her actions.

"I want you to be my first," Selena murmured and observed as his cheeks became a bit scarlet.

"I umm... Like... right now? Are you sure?", Stiles mumbled and Selena chuckled playfully. Stiles glanced at her with a serious face, not wanting to miss any slightest response that may have informed him differently.

"Yes, right now. And then forever.", Selena said and realized that she had never been more confident about anything in her life.

Selena was lost in her thoughts as her head was resting on Stiles's chest, his arms embracing her body protectively.

"What are you thinking about?", Stiles asked and ran his fingers up and down her arm.

"I don't know. I believed that maybe everything makes sense now, that I finally arrived at where I belong. I still don't know whether I'm a more human, werewolf, or a moon goddess, but I can sense hope now.", Selena said while listening to the steady rhythm of Stiles's pulse.

"What would you be, if you could choose?", Stiles questioned curiously and glanced towards the ceiling of his chamber. While resting in his bed and hugging Selena close to him, he truly felt serenity and protection surrounding him for once.

"I'm not sure. When all of this began, I badly wanted to be a regular person. But my adopted mother was a witch and my original parents were werewolves. I don't think anymore that I'm intended to be a human, you know? Maybe my entire existence was so difficult and chaotic because I never intended to live this type of life." Selena felt Stiles nod faintly before she braced herself on her arms to gaze at him. Stiles grinned a bit and ran his fingers through her golden hair.

"What about you? What would you be if you could choose?", Selena questioned and thought about how wonderful Stiles was in her eyes. Stiles did not have any supernatural abilities yet still was extremely courageous. He was brilliant and devoted and without him, most of his buddies were probably dead already. He always tried to do the right thing, yet was still able to confess the errors he committed. Stiles held so much love and vitality within of him and he was never hesitant to display it. Stiles was the ideal human and Selena could never envision him as anything else.

"I guess I'm delighted to be human. When Peter was an alpha, he offered me the bite once. I don't wanna lie, I thought about it for a second but I'm pleased that I decided against it. Scott was destined to be a werewolf, just as you are intended to be something more powerful than a human. But me... I am designed to be human and I prefer it like that."

"I like you exactly the way you are.", Selena responded smiling and kissing him tenderly, knowing that she was absolutely falling for him.

"Well, I should take you home now. You and Derek should speak about a lot of stuff.", Stiles added and Selena sighed, knowing that he was correct anyhow. Just half an hour later, Selena opened the wide entrance to their apartment and was delighted by the sight of Scott, Isaac, Allison, Kira, and Peter.

"Did we miss a pack meeting?", Selena inquired and proceeded into the loft as she heard Stiles locking the door before following her inside.

"I was at Stiles home to fetch you, but you were... occupied.", Scott murmured as Selena felt her cheeks flaming. For a brief while, she considered letting Derek remain human, believing it would be better for all of them if he did not have extraordinary powers of hearing and smell.

"So what's up?", Selena inquired again, attempting to play it calm. She came over to Derek who was resting on the table as he normally did.

"It's the Alpha. We discovered what he is and what he wants. Peter followed and observed him the previous several weeks." Scott explained and proceeded a step further.

"There's one issue, however.", Isaac added and Selena instantly felt everyone's eyes on her

Selena sought to absorb Scott's power for two days. She became stronger with every effort, but it still wasn't enough. She was ambitious, but her pals suggested it would be nice to take a vacation. A respite that would last longer than just one night. After Stiles had once expressed her normal-things-I-wanna-do-list, Lydia and Kira had been all over it. With Lydia's aid, Derek authorized them to host a tiny party in their loft this weekend. It was a full moon, so Scott and Isaac but probably stay out in the loft regardless.

"Are Scott and Isaac going to freak out because of the full moon?", Selena inquired while linking her fingers with the ones of Stiles. Stiles sighed deeply before kissing Selena's head.

"Nah, they are both skilled at managing themselves. If there was the least possibility of them panicking out, Derek would have tied them up already.", he said and Selena giggled, making Stiles's lips curl into a grin.

"Shall we go downstairs and arrange things for the party?", Stiles inquired and disengaged himself from Selena to get out of her bed.

"No, wait.", Selena murmured and grabbed his shirt to pull him back on the bed. The blonde girl laid back down, pulling Stiles down with her before kissing him. Stiles kissed her back but stopped when he felt her hands wander underneath his t-shirt, traveling up and down his chest.

"I... don't do that. Your brother is downstairs.", Stiles mumbled uncomfortably and Selena giggled.

"Are you terrified of him?" Selena lifted her eyebrows and grinned. Waiting for his response as her hands continued caressing his body.

"Are you kidding me? He's frightening me to death.", Stiles whispered and ultimately grabbed out for Selena's wrists to halt her motions. Selena laughed again and rolled her eyes playfully. She let Stiles rise and got out of the bed after him.

"Fine. Later then.", she winked before stepping out of her room. Stiles followed her downstairs and helped her to prepare the drinks and food for their guests. Derek did his best to ignore the recently adolescent pair and hoped, that he would get accustomed to it sooner or later. He left the loft shortly after, informing Selena that he'd be back after midnight and threatening Stiles, that he would kill him if they would break anything.

While they waited for their friends to arrive, Stiles and Selena sat on the couch and talked. Selena talked and Stiles listened. The girl finally felt comfortable enough around him and the others, to open up. While Selena told Stiles everything she had gotten to know about her family and werewolves, Stiles just sat there and admired her. Actually, he admired her happiness.

Scott, Kira, Lydia, Allison, and Isaac arrived shortly after the sun had set. Lydia was used to bigger parties, but for Selena's comfort, who didn't know any other people yet and had just started to trust them, she said yes for the mini party anyway. And even if it was just them, it was nice. They had fun and for a time, everything was fantastic. Everyone felt terrific. For a few hours, they were average teens who got drunk together. Lydia and Selena were dancing as Kira tried herself as a DJ. Allison and Isaac played Beerpong against Stiles and Scott. It didn't make sense, since only one member of each squad became truly intoxicated but even that didn't stop anybody from having fun. Allison nailed the final cup and yelled loudly. Stiles groaned and accepted the cup, swallowing the beer with one gulp. Just as he set the empty cup back down, he felt two arms snake over his tummy. He turned around and glanced down to see Selena beaming up at him.

"Having fun?", he simply said and put one of his palms on her face. Selena nodded and reached out for his hand.

"Come with me.", she said and interlaced their fingers before tugging Stiles with her. Stiles let his eyes travel around the room swiftly and noticed that everyone was occupied with something and having fun. He smiled lightly and followed Selena to her room, closing the door behind him. Just when Stiles wanted to pull her closer to him, Selena suddenly let go off his hand and pressed her hands on her ears, her face grimacing in pain.

"Selena? You ok?", Stiles inquired and took a step nearer, staring at her with anxiety in his eyes.

"Turn it off!", Selena cried and shook her head slowly while tugging her hair, her eyes were still shut in anguish.

"What? What is it?", Stiles said hesitantly and peered around the room. He startled a bit as Selena suddenly glanced up at him, her eyes sparkling golden.

"Turn off the music!", she yelled again and rubbed her hands over her face. Stiles tried to reach out for her but pulled away, as Selena hissed at him with fangs showing out. Stiles opened the door and yelled for Scott. Just a second later, the music went off and Scott ran up the stairs to Selena's room. Stiles turned around to Selena again, but his eyes trailed off to the window behind her. It was the full moon.

CHAPTER 14

"What the hell is happening to me?!", Selena shouted and grabbed at her hair again. Everything immediately felt different. Her senses had suddenly heightened by many times. Selena recognized odors she had never smelt before and heard sounds that no human should hear and she couldn't sort any of those things in her head. Every new emotion, fragrance, or noise pattered on her like raindrops, enveloping her entire body.

"You're changing. Call Derek.", Scott muttered and gazed at Stiles for a second, before going back to Selena. Stiles nodded and dialed Derek's number while exiting the room to walk downstairs.

"Scott, I... I can't stop it.", Selena abruptly murmured, when her entire blood started to boil. She glanced at Scott with golden eyes, as her chest rose and fell swiftly. Her entire body filled with wrath and she could feel it flood through her veins. It seemed like her entire body was screaming at her to let go, to go furious and destroy everything and everyone in this room.

"What's going on?", Selena suddenly heard a light voice and turned around to find Allison and Isaac standing inside her room. Selena gazed at Allison and snarled, looking at her with golden eyes. Allison jumped gently and moved back, letting Selena know that she was terrified. Selena fought hard to deny her emotions, but every predator manipulated their victims dread. She snarled again, advancing towards Allison before she was stopped by Scott jumping in front of her, shouting at her.

"Selena, stop!", he yelled and glared her down with angry eyes.

"Use your anchor.", Scott instructed her, but Selena fought to break free from his hold, hissing at him viciously. Selena observed as Isaac and Allison exited the room and her body prompted her to go after them. Scott still held her in place.

"Selena, use your anchor!", Scott urged again, but this time, it was an order. Selenas face turned to face Scott and she felt like obeying. Her mind went blank for a second before she played the memories of Stiles in her head like a movie. Selena slowly gained back control over her body and managed to finally sort all of the new sensations. Scott and Selena both turned around when they heard a loud shattering, followed by the loud noise of the alarming system going off. Selena heard people shouting for Scott and Isaac snarling, shortly after that, she recognized Stiles's voice screaming in anguish. Scott rushed downstairs, while Selena instantly felt numb. While her senses had been going wild before, they now concentrated exclusively on one thing. Selena stood there paralyzed, listening to Stiles's pulse, which was racing much too fast. She smelt a strange stench, but she was convinced, that it was blood. She heard yelling, shouting, and snarling, but she couldn't make out the voices. When someone yelled her name, Selena managed to go back to reality and fled the room. Only to be confronted by the alpha. The alpha grabbed the considerably smaller female by her neck and forced her down the steps brutally. Selena's head smacked the floor and she could feel how a wound developed and rapidly sought to heal again. The girl attempted to rise, but before her feet could hit the ground, the alpha had her back by her neck. Selena struggled in his hands and clutched for his arms, attempting to remove his abilities, but not the least thing occurred.

"I'm sorry, honey, but those few minutes of a full moon reaching its pinnacle, even moon gods are just regular werewolves. And something tells me, that I did my research a lot better than you did.", the alpha growled cruelly and extended his arm out so that Selena's feet couldn't touch the ground longer and she began to battle for oxygen. The alpha roared and let her fall to the ground, when suddenly the lights above them shattered, followed by cracking glass pouring down on them. Selena fell to her knees and struggled for oxygen. She glanced up and saw Kira standing in front of the alpha with flaming eyes. Kira ripped off her belt and slammed it down, holding a blade in her hands straight after. Kira fought the alpha with the sword, while Isaac attempted to aid with his claws. The alpha pulled Kira aside, throwing her into a wall forcefully. Isaac and Scott fought to keep back the alpha, as Selena jumped up and raced to Kira to aid her. Selena didn't even reach the black-haired girl when the alpha grabbed her again. She could feel his nails on her back and how they created deep scrapes. Selena went back down to the floor as the alpha caught hold of her ankle, dragging her towards him. He stepped over her and lifted his hand, preparing to cut her neck with his claws. Selena glanced at the alpha with horror in her eyes and was convinced, that her life would end in less than three seconds. Isaac and Scott were quicker, however, each of them ripping at one of his arms. Selena sprang to her feet swiftly as she suddenly heard gunfire. A second shot rang fired before the alpha fell. Selena spun around to find Derek and Mr. Argent standing at the doorway, each holding a revolver in their hands. They both moved to the left and assisted Isaac and Scott to chain up the alpha. Selena breathed in and out deeply before she knew what had just transpired. She glanced around the room and watched how Lydia attempted to aid Kira and how Allison kneeled next to Stiles.

Selena hurried up to Stiles and could hear her own heart shattering, as she saw him sprawled on the ground. His complexion was pale and his face was drenched in perspiration, while his t-shirt was covered in blood. He covered the cut with his palms, while Allison pushed down on his hands to stop the blood.

"Wha-what happened?", Selena stammered and began to fear. She kneeled next to him and sensed her hands beginning to tremble. The aroma of Stiles's blood was intense, making Selena feel nauseated. She focussed on his pulse again, knowing that it was slower than normal. There was so much blood. Way too much. Selena sat down on the chilly floor and drew Stiles towards her, placing his head on her lap. She called for Scott, who was next to them right after, looking down at Stiles with big eyes.

"Scott, you have to bite him.", Selena wailed and stared at Scott with tears flowing down her face. Scott scowled and gazed at her with an expression, that Selena couldn't decipher.

"Selena, I...", he slowly began and Selena shook, her head, knowing what he was about to say.

"Scott, he's dying! I know you can smell it, I know you can feel it because I can!"

"He doesn't want to be a werewolf, Selena.", Scott remarked calmly and stared at Selena with begging eyes. Selena shook her head again and wiped some of her tears.

"I- I know. But I can take the power again, once he has healed. I can do it. We can rescue him.", Selena muttered hesitantly and gazed down at Stiles.

"But you have to pass it on to someone else.", Allison reminded her gently and glanced at the blonde girl attentively.

"I don't care! Scott, just do it!", Selena yelled and Scott inhaled deeply before bending down. He carefully took his best friend's arm and looked at him before he bit him. Stiles muscles tensed and his eyes squeezed shut in pain. Selena grabbed his head and ran her fingers through his hair softly.

"He can shift, right? He can heal. Right?", Selena asked and looked back at Scott, whose eyes had filled with worry and tears.

"I don't know.", Scott said and clasped Stiles's hand in his own. Selena gazed outside the window and realized that the moon departed its peak. She sensed how she slowly returned to being human, her powerful senses and rage departing her body. Selena lost the aroma of blood in her nose and the sound of beating in her ears and she began to feel weak.

"Selena.", she heard Derek say gently and turned her head to look at her brother approaching her. He glanced at her with sorrowful eyes, before he put one hand on her shoulder. Selena saw how Scott wiped away some tears before he squeezed Stiles's hand. She glanced up and noticed Isaac turning around to face the wall as Kira grabbed Lydia's hand.

"W-wrong?", what's Selena faltered and stared at her pals.

"I can't hear his heartbeat anymore.", Scott answered and let go off Stiles's hand.

"No. No, no, no. You bit him, he needs to change.", Selena whispered again and laid her head on Stiles.

"Sel...", Allison said and laid her arm on Selena's shoulder tenderly. Selena shook her head and forced her eyes tight, making the scorching tears in her eyes fall. She raised her head and moved her head to gaze at the alpha, who was still bound up to a stake. He was barely awake, the wolfsbane weakening his body. Selena felt the fire within her body rise again and stood up. She moved up to the alpha and kneeled in front of him. She closed her eyes and exhaled deeply before she opened them again, staring at the alpha with silver eyes and grabbing his arms. Selena could feel his body tense and feel the energy flooding through her veins. Her veins felt like they were on fire, and her lungs felt like they were full of water. Selena began to feel disoriented, so she increased her grasp on the alpha's arms and battled the sense of burning and drowning. The blonde girl could feel how the alpha getting weaker, when she couldn't feel a pulse anymore, she let go off his arms. Selena fell backward, then turned her head when she heard someone utter Stiles's name. Scott pulled Stiles's shirt, displaying the wound that quickly began to heal. Stiles breathed in deeply and opened his eyes. Golden eyes. Selena staggered back and let herself collapse next to Stiles.

"Stiles. It's going to be ok.", she whispered and ran her fingers through his hair once again. Selena could sense how the force within her made her weak. She couldn't completely breathe or see or think and she knew, that she had to give it to Derek soon if she wanted to live.

"Selena, you have to pass the power to Derek, it's killing you!", Allison screamed but got held back by Isaac.

"When Derek is an alpha again, then I can't help Stiles anymore.", Selena whispered and stared at Stiles's wound, waiting for it to heal completely. The wound healed and Stiles breathed out. He was still weak but at least, he wasn't in any agony anymore. Selena lunged out for his arms but was stopped by someone restraining her wrists.

"Don't. It will kill you. It's alright like that." Selena gazed down at Stiles. He attempted to accept the truth, that he was going to be a werewolf. Trying to make a choice, but Selena had made it long before him.

"I'm not going to be the one who imposed this choice on you.", Selena muttered and pulled away from his embrace, grabbing for his arms straight after to seize what was not intended to be his. It didn't hurt. It was like sinking into a deep slumber. Like to be conscious of the final breath of air, before falling asleep. Stiles fell asleep, once the power had left his body again and Selena attempted to rise.

"Derek.", she murmured, but it sounded more like an order. Derek was at her side right after, holding her, so she wouldn't fall. The last thing Selena did was to lay her hands on his chest, to finally give him back, what belonged to him. She felt the alpha's strength leave her body, leaving Stiles' power back to slowly kill her. That was her last thought before peaceful darkness surrounded her.

Selena felt a comforting kind of warmth around her and slowly opened her eyes. She was resting on comfortable grass and glanced up to a crystal-clear sky. In the corner of her eye, she noticed a light shimmering. Curious to discover what it was, the girl rose and wandered across the green grass. While the grass tickled her bare legs, Selena kept moving forward with the light. Comfort and warmth come from it.

"Selena." Selena spun around, the white dress she was wearing fluttering around her body.

"Mum!", Selena answered, as she noticed her mother standing on the opposite side of the field. The blonde girl started running as fast as she could. For a short second, she thought that her mother would just vanish into the air, but suddenly, she found herself in her mother's arms.

"What are you doing here?", Selena asked happily and wrapped her arms around her mother's torso, squeezing her tightly. Her mother massaged the golden hair of her tiny daughter before breaking the embrace to gaze at her. Selena did the same. She looked just like she remembered her mother. The reddish-brown curls that fell on her shoulders just perfectly and her green eyes, sparkling with pure happiness.

"The question is, what are you doing here?", Selena heard another voice say. A voice, she got to meet initially not too long ago. Selena turned her head to see Talia heading up to them.

"I-I don't know. Where are we?"

"Your subconscious. It's like a world between life and death. Scott took you into the one of Derek once.", Talia stated and Selena finally understood.

"I gave Derek the power of the alpha. But I couldn't give him the power of Stiles as well.", Selena whispered gently and bowed her head, as she saw her mother grin slightly.

"Was it, because you were not able to, or because you didn't want to?", her mother inquired quietly and put a palm on Selena's pale face. She had always seen straight through her falsehoods.

"Stiles remarked, that I was supposed to be something more than a person. But I think that death was destined for me. I was born a moon goddess, as someone whose own power may destroy me. Then I was human and I was supposed to die inside this fire with you and dad. And if I would have been a werewolf, I would have been supposed to die in the fire with you. I'm not intended to live.", Selena answered frankly and let her gaze drift between her mother and Talia. Wherever Selena was right now, she felt tranquility for the first time in forever. She recalled all the awful things, but she didn't feel the anguish anymore. She felt liberated.

"My darling, you survived all of that, because you are supposed to have a far grander life than any of us. You have a brother now. He's your kin and you both are supposed to carry on the Hales tradition. There was a purpose, that you and Derek both survived those disasters." Selena nodded while feeling her mother tracing her fingers over her cheeks softly. Selena thought about Derek, how they both were the only family they had left now. She thought about Stiles and how she had just begun to fall for him. And she thought of Scott, Allison, Kira, Isaac, and Lydia and how they had sacrificed their lives only to rescue hers. Selena understood, that abandoning them would be wrong. Dying would be selfish.

While she stood in the comforting light of death, she suddenly understood, that it was not an end she was craving for. It was a fresh beginning.

"Go back now, darling.", Talia said and took Selena's hand in her own.

"How? I didn't pass Stiles power. It's too late."

"Then take it on your own. Fight your goddess and become a werewolf. And then, you go back." Selena nodded and took the hand of her mother, squeezing both hands of the elder woman before closing her eyes. She could feel their presence vanish and knew it was time to become a werewolf.

"Stiles? What the heck are you doing here? Don't you have to go to school or something?", Derek said with annoyance in his voice, as he opened the door to a worried Stiles. Derek wiped the sleep out of his eyes and Stiles could see that he was exhausted.

"I... I didn't sleep the entire night and I just...", Stiles attempted to explain but Derek already knew what the youngster intended to say.

Selena still hadn't woken up and to say that Stiles and Derek were growing nervous, was an underestimate.

"Go and care after her. After that have some sleep, you may remain here.", Derek remarked and then departed to get some more sleep. Stiles merely nodded and went into the apartment before locking the door behind him. He climbed up the stairs and cautiously entered Selena's room. Stiles always tried to be as cautious and quiet as possible, just as he was frightened to wake her awake. Even though he knew, that she probably wouldn't wake up very soon.

After Selena had passed out that night, they instantly rushed her to the hospital. Misses McCall had assured them, that she was completely fine though and that she just was in a deep sleep. She had sent them home with the words "that's a supernatural problem you have to deal with."

Deaton was sure, that Selena was fighting an inner battle. Something similar to what happened with Stiles and the Nogitsune. He said that she would wake up, whenever she was ready and her mind would win the battle. Until then, she would stay sleeping beauty.

"Just wake up, please. We need you. Derek, Kira, Allison... I need you. Come back to me, ok?", Stiles said and prayed, that Derek wouldn't listen to him. Derek had done everything to rouse her awake, he even wanted to go into her thoughts but Deaton had instructed him to allow her some time. It had been four days since then and nothing had changed. Stiles knew that it was only a matter of time before Derek would flip out and simply step into her thoughts. Stiles groaned and stroked his fingers through her light blonde hair when his fingers abruptly stopped moving. He took a strand of hair and delicately stroked it between his fingers. It was dark brown. Nearly black.

"What the hell?", he mumbled and ran his fingers up and down the strand of dark brown hair.

"Derek?!", he yelled and heard the door open only a few seconds later. Derek stepped over to Stiles and glanced at him with a puzzled gaze.

"Since when does she have that?", Stiles said and gazed back down at the strand of hair that was still between his fingers. Derek followed his eyes and inclined his head before approaching closer.

"I don't know.", he said and Stiles took his hand back from Selena as Derek combed his hands through her hair to see if he would discover more of the dark brown strands.

"My mother commented, that her blue eyes and her light hair were somewhat like her metamorphosis. It's the look of a moon goddess.", Derek remarked and softly caressed Selena's face before he let his hand fall back down to his side.

"Do you think she's losing her power?", Stiles said as Derek shrugged his shoulders.

"Maybe. I'll go and chat with Deaton. Are you remaining or going to school?"

"I'm staying.", Stiles responded and gazed back down at Selena. Derek merely nodded and exited the room. Stiles heard the door to the loft being opened and closed and yawned, feeling sleep tugging on him. He kissed Selena's forehead and headed to the living room to catch up on some sleep.

"Stiles. Stiles, wake up." Stiles woke in his sleep and twisted around. He blinked a few times to find Isaac and Scott peering down at him.

"Where's Derek? Is everything ok?", Scott inquired and Stiles nodded. He extended his arms out and sat up straight before running his hands over his face.

"Yeah, he went to grab Deaton. Something is occurring with Sel..."

"Stiles!", he heard Allison's voice coming from Selena's room. Without thinking twice, Scott and Stiles leaped to their feet and rushed up the stairs. Isaac followed his buddies and ran directly into them until they unexpectedly halted at the doorway.

"What the heck is happening?", Allison questioned and pointed at Selena. The three lads gently moved farther into the room. Scott and Isaac both gazed at Selena with anxiety in their eyes, while Stiles took a few steps closer to the sleeping girl. Only a few strands of her light blonde hair were left, leaving the girl with virtually full black hair. Her typically pale complexion didn't look so white anymore and Stiles wondered if her sparkling blue eyes had also altered their hue.

"It began this morning. Derek went to retrieve Deaton. We believe that maybe, she's losing her abilities.", Stiles stated and glanced at Allison who had a pout on her face.

"I don't understand it. She simply opted to not be the moon goddess anymore, or what? How does it even work?", Isaac questioned as Scott shook his shoulders before he heard footsteps getting closer. He turned around and saw

Deaton and Derek entering the room a few seconds later.

"It's not about selecting. It's more about battling. A struggle between the wolf and the goddess of the moon.", Deaton stated and briefly nodded to welcome everyone. Allison and Stiles stood back allowing Deaton to take a closer look at Selena.

"Wolf? What wolf, she's not a werewolf.", Allison inquired and Deaton turned his head to gaze at her with a tiny grin on his lips.

"That's correct. At least not yet. On the night of the full moon, Selena absorbed the abilities of two werewolves. The one of the alpha and the one of Stiles. We assumed that she handed it to Derek, but I suppose that really, she could only give him one of both. Which indicates that Stiles' strength is still inside her." Deaton explained and everyone appeared to think about it.

"But didn't Talia say that it would kill her? If she won't give it to someone?", Allison inquired again and Deaton nodded.

"Right. I feel that Selena is attempting to take it herself. It's against nature to be both. Werewolf and a moon goddess. The goddess is her nature, however, her subconsciousness, and I suppose that half is struggling against the wolf. Selenas awareness is the wolf however, the part she consciously picked, is the part she wants to be. And it appears like this portion is winning." Deaton grinned again and allowed his sight to travel across the room. Everyone appeared to relax and suddenly, everything looked quiet.

"She looks precisely like Laura, don't you think?", Deaton remarked and laid a hand on Derek's shoulder. Derek only nodded and wiped his tears with the back of his palms.

"Alright, now let's give her some time. Derek will call you when she's awake." Derek happily nodded and grabbed the chair that was in front of the desk. He dragged it nearer the bed and sat down, ready to wait for Selena to wake up.

Stiles, Allison, Scott, and Isaac followed Deaton outside the room. They were still anxious, but their hearts felt so much lighter. Selena would wake up and when she did, we would finally know who she was.

Thank You For Reading

Michael E. Sweeny